AUTHOR'S NOTE

There are several modern royals in India. But for the sake of my story, the royals, and their territories that I have used, are all part of my imagination. While the places Udaipur, Jodhana and Indore exist, the kingdoms, palaces and the characters do not exist outside my imagination.

Books by Sundari Venkatraman

Standalone novels
The Malhotra Bride
Meghna
The Madras Affair
An Autograph for Anjali
Twin Torment
Finding Anya
Mr. Perfect
Man Friday
Her Prince Charming
Love in Agartha
Arjun's Penance
The Floundering Author
Once Bitten Twice Lucky
Ryan Finds a Bride
Tinder Loving Care
Shaan Gets Hitched
For Better or For Worse
Heartthrob
Call of the Heart
Sing For Me

Collection of shorts
Matches Made in Heaven
Tales of Sunshine

The Groom Series Trilogy
#1 Groomnapped
#2 Gobsmacked
#3 Grounded

Dashavatar (Indian Mythology)
MATSYA: The First Avatar
KURMA: The Second Avatar
VARAHA: The Third Avatar
NARASIMHA: The Fourth Avatar
VAMANA: The Fifth Avatar
PARASHURAMA: The Sixth Avatar

The Writer's Toolkit (Non-fiction)
Publishing Your Book on Amazon KDP

Marriages Made in India Series
#1 The Runaway Bridegroom
#2 Her Smitten Husband
#3 His Drunken Wife
#4 Her Secret Husband
#5 The Casanova's Wife
#6 Her Bohemian Husband

The Bansal Legacy Trilogy
#1 Simha International
#2 Rose Garden International
#3 Maharaja International

Written in the Stars Series
#1 Scorpio Superstar
#2 Leo's Desire
#3 Taurus Temptation
#4 Virgo's Krush

The Thakore Royals Trilogy
#1 The Marriage Predicament
#2 Tied in Knots
#3 The Wooing of the Shrew

Romantic Shorts
#1 Chahti Hoon Tumhe
#2 Beauty is but Skin Deep
#3 Madeinheaven.com
#4 An Arranged Match
#5 The Reluctant Bride
#6 Shweta ka Swayamvar
#7 Papa's Girl
#8 Red Rose Dating Agency
#9 Rahat Mili
#10 Reema's Matchmakers
#11 The Matchmaker's Dream

The Princess Series
(Historical Romance)
#1 The Passionate Princess
#2 The Rebel Princess

"Princess…" Rajvardhan buried his face in her shoulder, placing tender kisses along the slope, his breath coming in soft gasps. She looked lovely with her soft curls tumbling all over her shoulders and back, her dark eyes still smudged with sleep, though he couldn't miss the burgeoning desire peeping through.

"Raj…" Chitrangada protested weakly, her body closing the small distance between them as it seemed to have a mind of its own as it refused to follow her order to stay away from the sinful temptation that was presented to her that morning.

She forgot her own name when he closed his lips over hers, catching the sound of his name as he kissed her. First softly, his mouth brushing light as a feather over her trembling lips. Then slowly, the tip of his tongue reaching out to trace the pouting shape. Then thoroughly as he drew her lower lip into his mouth, sucking on it slowly and deeply, making her moan with want. "Raj…"

ABOUT THE AUTHOR

Sundari Venkatraman is an Indie Author who has 61 books to her credit. These books have consistently featured in the Top 100 Bestseller Lists on Amazon Kindle, in both romance as well as Asian Drama categories. Her latest hot romances have all been on #1 Bestseller slot in Amazon India for over a month.

TIED IN KNOTS is the second book in The Thakore Royal trilogy; and based on Indian Contemporary Royals. This kindle book remained in #1 Bestseller position on Amazon India for four months from its release in both the Contemporary Romance and Asian Drama categories.

Even as a child, Sundari absolutely loved the 'lived happily ever after' syndrome and she grew up on a steady diet of fairy tales, Phantom comics and Mandrake comics. It was always about good triumphing over evil and a happy ending after the protagonists surmounted all unexpected obstacles.

Once she entered her teens, Sundari switched her loyalties from fairy tales to Mills & Boon. While she loved reading both of these, she kept visualising what would have happened if there were similar situations happening in India; to local heroes and heroines. And of course, the joy of vanquishing the ubiquitous evil villains! Her imagination soared and she happily ensconced herself in a rosy romantic cocoon for many years.

Then came the writing—a true bolt from the blue! And Sundari Venkatraman has never looked back.

T I E D
in
K N O T S

THE THAKORE ROYALS
BOOK 2

SUNDARI VENKATRAMAN

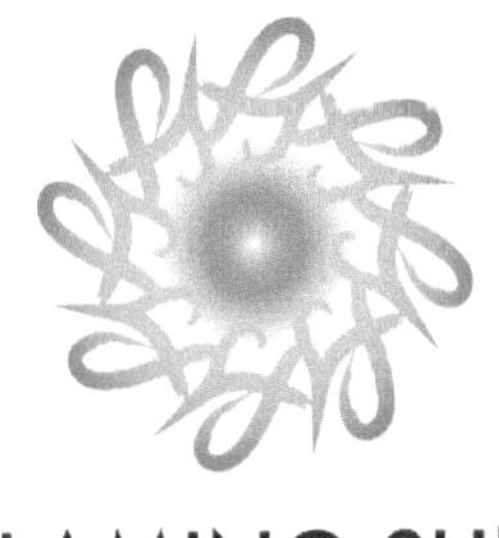

FLAMING SUN

Notion Press Media Pvt Ltd

No. 50, Chettiyar Agaram Main Road,
Vanagaram, Chennai, Tamil Nadu – 600 095

First Published by Flaming Sun 2018
Printed & Distributed by Notion Press
Copyright © Sundari Venkatraman 2023
All Rights Reserved.

ISBN 979-8-88975-567-8

Edited by: Preeti Arora
Beta Read by: Rubina Ramesh
Cover Illustration: Unaiza Merchant
Launched by: The Book Club

DEDICATION

To Women Power

Princess Chitrangada Vasudeva looked out of the window of her limousine as her driver brought it to a halt at the signal. The snow that had begun as a drizzle was thickening and had all the makings of a blizzard.

Without pausing and not bothering to think, she pushed the door open to get out of the car and rushed across the road towards the pavement on the opposite side, the heels of her calf length black boots tap-tapping as she ran. Luckily for her, her bodyguards were following her in another vehicle which was further at the back, at least twenty cars away. She jogged in the opposite direction, so focussed on getting away that she did not feel the cold despite wearing a sleeveless evening gown. Of course, the four pegs of white rum that she had consumed also helped. She gathered the folds of her red velvet dress in a slender hand, holding it up to mid-calf, her other hand gripping her clutch. She refused to look back as she rushed headlong, a triumphant grin on her face as she put distance between herself and her four bodyguards.

She turned around the corner near River Limmat in Zurich and continued to walk speedily, uncaring that it was past midnight and she wasn't even sure where she was going. Just now, Chitrangada's aim was to escape her jailors. Yes, that is what her bodyguards were, men who had been appointed by her father, Raja Bikram Vasudeva of Jodhana in Rajasthan, to keep her safe.

Safe from what? That is exactly what she didn't understand. There was no threat to her life. It wasn't as if her father had so much money that she might be kidnapped for ransom. Then why the hell did she need, not one but four hefty thugs—well, that is what the bodyguards seemed to her—to guard her?

It was to keep her in line, ensuring that she had no way of escape from her father's horrendous plans for her. If he had had his way, Chitrangada wouldn't be in Zurich today, but closeted in their palace home in Jodhana fort.

She almost ran now, her heels tapping against the pavement rhythmically, even as her heart pumped harder than ever. When the silence struck her suddenly, muffled by the thickly falling snow, Chitrangada stopped to catch her breath, holding on to her side with her right hand, rubbing at the stitch that she hadn't even been aware of having while she had been running for almost twenty minutes. She turned around to see if anyone was following her and another grin split her face when she found herself all alone, with no human being within sight. That the snow had made visibility poor was actually a good thing. This way, her father's henchmen would never find her, at least not easily.

Good! It would serve them right when they had to deliver the news to Raja Bikram that they had lost track of the princess's whereabouts. She imagined her father's panic when the phone rang to give him the news but felt no remorse. It was nothing more than what he deserved.

She stood straight and looked up at the skies and laughed softly when the snowflakes fell all the harder, not giving a thought to the fact that she was totally stranded in the middle of Zurich with only a clutch that carried her driver's license and the key to her hotel room, along with a few hundred Euros.

Chitrangada began to feel cold all of a sudden, realising finally that she had left her full-length coat of faux fur in her limousine, along with her cell phone.

Drat!

She had no plans to return to her suite at Hotel Storchen. She had some money, just enough to maybe get a room in some small hotel. If only she had her phone with her, it would have helped her navigate her way around the European city. But then again, if she had had her phone, she would have been caught and hauled back to her hotel by now.

It was all for the best!

Princess Chitrangada really didn't think so after an hour of walking from hotel to hotel, trying to find accommodation. The money she had wasn't of much use in securing her a room, even if the amount wasn't small. They didn't want to give her a room as she didn't have her passport with her.

Why was the world full of bastards!

Prince Rajvardhan Thakore of Udaipur drove his car down the road, trying to find his hotel. He looked at his phone, trying to gauge the distance to Alden Suite Hotel Splügenschloss Zurich where he was booked for a couple of nights. Raising his head from his phone, just before accelerating, he hit the brake suddenly as he stared in fascination at the woman who appeared out of nowhere. The lady in red stepped in front of his car, both her arms up in the air as she waved to him. Rajvardhan stared open-mouthed at the gorgeous figure. Was she for real?! She couldn't be human. How could she be if she could stand out there under the falling snow in a sleeveless evening gown?

Unable to resist, he got out of his car to walk over to her.

"Hi!" she said, her voice breathless as Chitrangada looked at the man who stepped out of the car that she had stopped. He was so obviously Indian. Should she be grateful for that? Or wary? Shaking her head, she continued, "I need help. I'm stranded."

"Hi!" Rajvardhan stared at the vision in front of him, fascinated despite himself. It took him but a few minutes to register her slim, but luscious figure, the black-as-coal eyes her best feature in a face alive with vigour. Her cheeks were flushed a deep pink while her long, curling lashes—they were so real too—fluttered as she pinned him with her gaze. "Would you like me to drop you to your hotel? Get in." Used to giving orders, Rajvardhan had to tone down his haughty voice.

Chitrangada shook her head. "No. I don't have a room. I…"

Rajvardhan sighed impatiently. She didn't appear lost or poor by any means, not with the necklace of rubies which graced her slender throat. How was it possible for her to be stranded on the streets of Zurich without a room? Was she conning him? But then, he couldn't just leave her standing there in the middle of the road, past midnight, especially as it was snowing so heavily. "Get in the car and we'll talk." This time, the order was obvious. He turned to get into the driver's seat on the left, not waiting to see if she followed him.

With a frown and an explicit oath, Chitrangada got into the passenger seat, shivering as a blast of hot air hit her cold body. Men!

"Here." Rajvardhan removed a woollen rug from the back of his car and handed it over to her. "This will keep you warm. I don't have a towel though." He sat back in his seat as if he had all the time in the world, while he waited for her to get comfortable.

Well… he isn't so bad, after all, thought Chitrangada as she wrapped the rug around herself, before warming her hands at the heater.

"How come you're walking the streets of Zurich at this hour? And alone too. Are you from India? Or maybe an NRI?"

She raised a hand as if to shut him off, her gesture regal. Couldn't he ask one question at a time? She glared at him; her charcoal gaze fiery as she took in his handsome looks. She felt compelled to change her mind about him. *Arrogant!* That is what he was, if she needed to describe him in one word.

"I'm an Indian, visiting Zurich. I… I don't have a room to go to. I've lost my passport as well as my cell phone." Chitrangada looked down at her hands, unable to meet his sharp brown gaze. She couldn't blame him if he thought she was a complete idiot. Tch! But did it really matter? She was free of her bodyguards, wasn't she? And—she bent her head to hide the wide grin that threatened to split her face in two—wasn't she lucky to land up with a guy who appeared rather decent? He had even offered her a rug to keep her warm. Maybe he could get her a room in the hotel where he was put up. Money wasn't an issue.

"Do you want me to take you to the Indian Consulate in that case?" Rajvardhan looked at her bent head, fisting his hands as he felt a sudden urge to run his fingers through the silky tresses that were almost dry from the warmth inside the car.

Chitrangada's head came up with a jerk on hearing that. What the fuck?! Most definitely not. Her father and the consul general knew each other only too well. She valiantly hid the panic that peeped out of her eyes, before saying, "I can manage to get there by myself tomorrow morning. If only you could help me get a room at your hotel? I tried to do that myself. But they all refused me since I have no passport." Her voice was husky as she requested him, hating the idea of being dependent on a stranger's help. An arrogant one at that!

"What about your hotel room? They will surely let you in even if you don't have your passport?" His shrewd brown eyes looked piercingly into hers.

Shit! She hadn't thought of that. "I… I just arrived this evening," she said, not realising the depth of the pit she was digging herself into.

"Where's your luggage?" The question shot out of him like a whiplash when he looked her up and down as she sat huddled into the woollen rug.

Damn him! How many questions?! Can't a girl just get lost in a foreign city without being treated like a criminal? She thought fast on her feet. "I left them in a locker since I wanted to look around the city. And, before you ask me another question, I lost the key to the locker too." She glared at him defiantly. "Look here. I need a room for just tonight. I can pay for it. See." She opened her purse to show him the Euros she had tucked away there. "If only you could help me get one at your hotel." She would not plead, even if it meant that he was going to throw her back out on the street.

"What's your name?"

She was prepared for this one. "Princess." No way was she going to give him her real name. Chitrangada was a rather uncommon one. She did not want him to trace her on the internet. And she planned to remain incognito as long as she could.

Rajvardhan grinned despite his irritation. She was a con-artist, most definitely. What kind of a name was 'Princess'? But before he could voice his thoughts, she asked, "And yours?"

"I'm Raj."

"Thank you for rescuing me, Raj. Shall we go?"

"You thank me too soon," he said as he switched gears to drive the car forward. "It might be difficult to get a room during this season. Let us go find out."

"I'll keep my fingers crossed." The fire in her gaze disappeared as her eyes gleamed with mischief.

But it was the flash of dimples on her soft cheeks that caught Rajvardhan's attention as he pulled his gaze away from her face with an effort to keep it on the road. He really needed to concentrate as visibility was terribly poor by now.

He drove the car into the compound of his hotel, removing his leather jacket from the back of his car before stepping out. He handed the car keys to the concierge and requested him to remove his luggage from the boot before parking the car.

Rajvardhan turned around to watch Princess step out of the passenger's seat, the woollen rug still wrapped around her body, unable to stop the smile that broke out on his face. She had guts, for sure. "Shall we?" he called out to her, before holding his arm out.

Surprised yet again, Chitrangada placed her hand on his arm, walking beside him as they entered the hotel. Raj was a confusing man indeed. He seemed to have his chivalrous moments despite his rude manners. She mentally shrugged. What did it matter?! This was the first and last time she was going to set eyes on him, ever.

It wasn't long before Chitrangada realised that she had arrived at that erroneous conclusion too soon.

2

"What? You don't have even one empty suite?" Chitrangada stared open-mouthed at the receptionist. This was simply ridiculous. What was she to do now?

Rajvardhan pressed a hand on her shoulder, keen to stop her from talking any more. He immediately took his hand away as if burnt when he felt a sudden jolt of electricity. "Calm down, Princess," he said, his voice soft. He turned to the receptionist and said, "Could you make that two guests in my suite, please?"

Chitrangada couldn't help noticing that his French was flawless, without a trace of accent, unlike her heavily accented German. She had had to repeat herself a few times before the locals understood her. But what did he mean about two guests in his suite? "Listen…"

Rajvardhan turned to give her a warning look, a deep frown on his face. "I'm sure it can wait until we reach the privacy of our room, my darling, whatever it is that you want to tell me."

Chitrangada scowled at him ferociously, though she shut up. He was right. It was best that she dealt with him when they were alone, away from the receptionist's hearing. Or the chances were high that she would be thrown out of the hotel, what with neither passport nor luggage.

She walked with him to the elevator bank, following him into the lift, turning to look into the mirror. Looking at her, no one would believe that she had been walking on the wet streets of Zurich in the middle of the night. Her hair had dried up completely, luxurious and dark brown curls framing her oval face. Her startled black eyes connected with Rajvardhan's chocolatey gaze and she simply stared at him.

He was beyond handsome with his classical and clean-cut looks. The shadow of a fuzz darkened his flat cheeks that ended in a square and determined chin. His brown eyes were large, stopping short of appearing feminine only because of the short, thick eyelashes framing them. His eyebrows were dark and well-defined and the forehead above them was broad, thick strands of silky hair caressing it, making her hand itch to brush them back onto his head, where they belonged. Her gaze roved his face, refusing to return to meet his as she felt a sudden awareness engulfing her.

The doors swung open suddenly as the elevator stopped, making Chitrangada become aware of her surroundings. They walked down the luxurious corridor to reach the suite. The door was left open invitingly by the bellhop who was walking out of the bedroom after keeping Rajvardhan's luggage on a low table next to the wardrobe.

Rajvardhan thanked him before handing him a hefty tip, making the man smile and thank the guest profusely.

A fuming Chitrangada started yelling the moment the door shut behind the bellhop. "What the hell do you mean, telling the hotel that we'll share your room? How dare you…"

Rajvardhan turned away from her as he shrugged out of his suit jacket. "Do me a favour. Just get out of here and find your own room." His voice was gruff as he walked towards the bedroom. He was too tired to put up with her tantrums. He had been travelling since the past few days and had been sleeping on flights. He so needed a proper bed tonight as he was all set to crash.

Her jaw dropped. Whatever it was, she hadn't expected this from him, that he would be ready to throw her out of the suite. She walked behind him, her temper blowing out of control. "How dare you? How dare you insult me like this? What kind of a man are you that you are ready to throw your country woman out on the streets in the middle of the night? How…"

Rajvardhan turned around in a flash as he pulled off his tie and threw it on the back of a chair before unbuttoning his shirt, uncaring about her presence. "Can you just hear yourself, *Princess*?" He laid heavy stress on her name, his voice sarcastic, before continuing, "You say that I have great daring in offering to share my room with you. Then you contradict yourself insisting that I want to throw you out on the streets, that too with great daring. Come to a decision, woman. I can't be doing both."

He turned away, not bothering to wait for her answer as he removed the belt from his pants.

"Stop," she shouted, her eyes blazing fire as she stared fascinatedly at his tight butt. Would he dare to undress completely in front of her? Should she walk away to the sitting room? Chitrangada dug in her heels. No, she wouldn't. Why should she? It wasn't as if she hadn't seen men in swimming briefs. She folded her arms to stand right where she was, tapping her foot impatiently.

He turned again, pausing in the action of pulling down his fly. "What now?" he growled, his eyebrows coming together in a frown. He controlled his amusement as he caught the expression on her face. It looked like she couldn't help checking out his body at every opportunity; earlier in the lift, and now, right here in his bedroom.

"Raj, how can I share a room with you? We are strangers."

"Why didn't you think about that when you stopped my car out there?"

"But... but that was different. I was stranded on the streets without my passport or luggage. I couldn't just sleep in a park, not in the snow, could I?" Her voice was triumphant as she thought to win him over with her logic.

"You mean you aren't stranded now?" A shapely eyebrow went up in query again as he stepped out of his pants before walking towards the bathroom.

"Raj!" Her voice was a frustrated scream now. "How could you…?"

He turned around in a flash, making her eyes go wide when they landed on his magnificent chest. "Listen, *Princess*. I'm beat and need to sleep, like since yesterday. You are welcome to share the suite with me. As you can see, there are a lot of pillows and cushions. And there must be more sheets and comforters in the cupboard. You can use the sofa in the other room. If it goes against your propriety, you are welcome to just get out and leave me in peace." With those words, Rajvardhan left her right there and went into the bathroom.

Bastard! What kind of guy was he? He hadn't even bothered to offer her the use of the bathroom first. Chivalry be damned! Raj didn't even have common courtesy.

"I can hear you, Princess." Rajvardhan's voice came through, startling Chitrangada, as she noticed that the door to the bathroom wasn't completely shut. And she just now realised that she had spoken out loud. "For all you know, forget about being non-chivalrous, I could even be a rapist or an axe murderer. Think about it." There was laughter in his voice that was soon drowned by the sound of the shower.

Princess Chitrangada Vasudeva stamped her foot in fury. Axe murderer indeed. She will show him.

She sat down on a corner of the bed to pull off her boots, before getting up to gather all the stuff to create a makeshift bed for herself, sighing as her bare feet sank into the thick carpet. Going to the wardrobe, she removed a couple of sheets and a comforter and walked with them to the sitting room before dumping them on the sofa. She went back into the bedroom to pick a few pillows and a couple of cushions—if she had her way, she would have taken all the pillows away just so as to make him uncomfortable—and made her bed on the sofa. She stood back to check out her handy work. It did look comfortable if she was half a dozen inches shorter than the five feet, ten inches she was. Damn it! It promised to be a long night.

"The bathroom is all yours now." Rajvardhan called to her as he stepped out, wrapped in a towelling robe that fell a few inches above his knees.

Chitrangada shut her eyes tight for a few seconds before opening them to look at the floor, as she walked towards the bathroom.

"I presume you've decided to share my suite. Are you sure your royal reputation wouldn't be in shreds by tomorrow morning, Princess?"

She whirled around on her way to the bathroom and her eyes shot daggers at him. Had he guessed that she was a princess? But how could that be? Looking at his mischievous face, Chitrangada realised that he was needling her because of the name she had given him. "I can live with that," she muttered.

"Here, you might need these." Rajvardhan threw a full-sleeved t-shirt and a pair of pyjamas at her.

She caught them with expertise, her throat choking up as she felt forced to thank him. She had forgotten that she had no change of clothes. But he hadn't. No, that still didn't make him a nice person. He simply irritated the hell out of her. Chitrangada fled when she noticed him loosening the belt of his robe. She wasn't going to watch the floor show for sure.

It was a good fifteen minutes before she stepped out of the bathroom, clad only in the t-shirt that smelled of him—a musky perfume and all male. She wondered if she would be able to sleep with his perfume clinging to her. Stepping out, she saw that the lights were off in the bedroom as she tiptoed her way to the sitting room, shutting the door softly behind her.

Sleep failed to come as Rajvardhan lay on his back, the comforter drawn over his naked body, his hands stacked under his head. Princess! He was sure that wasn't her real name. *But she definitely has royal airs*, he thought, a smile on his face. She was beautiful, almost ethereally so, until you caught the aggression in her eyes that indicated that she was a rebel. A rebel princess! Her charcoal eyes glowed with joy, burned in anger, or danced with mischief, never still for a moment, capturing his attention completely. He had had a difficult time keeping his distance from her. But then, Prince Rajvardhan Thakore would never take advantage of a woman. For all her brave talk, he could see that she had been nervous about spending the night in his suite. He wondered about the actual truth. He didn't believe that she had no room booked in her name in the European city. Her story had been too tall to swallow. Rajvardhan grinned to himself, sure by now that she was playing truant. Now that, he could understand as he so loved to do it himself.

He got up to punch his pillows into a more comfortable shape before lying down again. But sleep continued to elude him. Maybe a glass of hot milk would help. The hotel had twenty-four hours room service. He got up to pull on a pair of shorts before walking into the sitting room. He had better check if Princess needed something too.

"Hey!"

Chitrangada fell off the sofa, startled to hear his voice. She had been tossing on her makeshift bed, doing her best to find a comfortable position, only to fail. She fitted on the sofa only if she pulled her knees close to her chest. But that was no inducement to sleep. And she had been sure that Raj must be out like the light. He had said that he was too tired and needed his beauty's sleep, hadn't he?!

What the hell was he doing here in her room now?

She got up from the floor, muttering curses in both Hindi and English as she rubbed a hand over her hip that had hit the floor. Not that anything more than her ego had been really hurt as the carpet was too thick.

"What do you want?" she asked him rudely, before sitting on the sofa with a plonk.

"I'm going to order some hot milk. Do you need anything from room service?"

Chitrangada brightened. "Can I have pizza? I just realised that I'm hungry. That's probably the reason I'm unable to sleep. Couldn't you sleep either?" She asked as an afterthought.

Rajvardhan bit his lip to stop himself from laughing. Somehow, he didn't think she would appreciate his amusement. She looked adorable in his t-shirt that fell to mid-thigh, her long, long legs appearing slim and sexy. Her hair was tumbled all over her face, making her appear cute. "That's right. Do you have a craving for some special topping, Princess? Or anything will do?" He went to the dining table and picked up the menu before handing it over to her.

Chitrangada watched him walk away from her, her eyes drawn to his strong, bare legs, the muscles rippling as he moved. It looked like he was blessed with way more than his share of good looks. "Do you think I can have chunks of chicken, onions and peppers, topped with loads of cheese?" She drooled as she thought of the pizza, her stomach growling. She had only munched on starters at the party she had been to, too distracted by thoughts of escaping her bodyguards to eat a proper dinner.

"Let me check," said Rajvardhan, lifting the receiver to call room service. "Would you like to drink something?"

"Wine?" She smiled, her dimples flashing, catching his gaze. She paused before talking again, "On second thoughts, I'll have coffee. I need something hot."

His eyebrow went up in query as he spoke into the phone, placing their orders. "Coffee then? Are you sure you won't change your mind again?" His eyes danced as he looked at her.

Chitrangada tried to glare at him but failed. *The situation is too surreal*, she thought as her lips curled in an inadvertent smile which made her eyes glow.

Rajvardhan placed the hand phone on its stand, staring at her dumbfounded. If anything, she appeared more beautiful than earlier. And he realised he liked his t-shirt on her, hugging her luscious curves. Realising that he was staring, he turned his gaze to the window and walked towards it, pushing back the curtains to look down at the near-empty road.

She cleared her throat loudly, trying to draw his attention. Failing, she called out, "Raj."

He turned his head halfway, refusing to move from his position. She was a walking temptation and he wanted to stay as far away as possible. "What?"

"Why don't you sit down? You seem threatening somehow, when you are on your feet." He must be a few inches above six feet for sure. Not that should really be threatening, considering that she was so tall herself. But Chitrangada had suddenly decided that she would like to know this handsome hunk some more. And she couldn't deny that he was considerate.

He hadn't found her request for pizza strange at all, despite it being half past two in the morning.

He sighed. Talk about temptation calling! She was literally calling out to him. Unable to resist, he walked over and sat on the bed she had made out of the sofa.

"I didn't exactly mean right there." Chitrangada muttered in a small voice, scowling in his direction. As it is, it had been difficult to get to sleep. Now, he was creating more memories by parking his butt on her bed.

"You're too demanding, Princess." There was laughter in Rajvardhan's voice as he looked up at her, patting the space next to him. "Why don't you sit down too? Unless it's your turn to take a threatening stance."

"Very funny." She didn't take up his invitation as she settled down on a single sofa adjacent to him. All that amount of bare, masculine skin and rippling muscles were getting to her. She gritted her teeth. *Why couldn't he wear something more than the briefest shorts on this side of the globe?* She thought, crossing her arms across her breasts as she felt them tightening, making her nipples pebble hard. She bit into her lower lip, working hard at controlling the sudden lure she felt towards the mind-blowingly handsome man sitting across from her.

The bell rang before he said anything in reply. Getting up immediately, he opened the door to let the waiter in.

"That smells so amazing," declared Chitrangada, getting up to sit on a dining chair, crossing one long leg over the other.

Rajvardhan couldn't help gazing at the length of her legs, even as his imagination flashed a scene in his mind's eye, that of those very same legs wrapped tightly around his waist as he took her. He sat down abruptly on the chair opposite hers, not wanting her to notice his tenting shorts. He poured a cup of milk for himself and raised it in a toast to her, his voice mocking as he said, "To you, Princess."

She wrinkled her sharp nose at him, saying, "Why don't you help yourself to some pizza? There's enough for two."

He shook his head, his eyes looking on in fascination as she bit into a slice of pizza with her teeth, his skin in goose bumps as he almost felt them against his skin. "Not for me, Princess. I can't sleep on a full stomach."

"Fussy, aren't we?" She made a face at him as she munched her way through another slice.

"Would you like me to pour you some coffee?" he asked, not really surprised at his reluctance to part company with her.

"You would?" Chitrangada stared at him, startled. He was too damn confusing. He was rude and then he was polite. Which was the real Raj?

"Obviously. I wouldn't have asked otherwise, would I?" He didn't wait for her reply as he poured coffee into a cup. "Do you take cream and sugar?"

"Yes please. Lots of cream and one sugar."

"Here you go." He added the cream and sugar, stirring the coffee vigorously with a spoon before handing her the cup.

She took a sip, closing her eyes to savour the coffee, the blissful expression on her face stirring his libido all the more. "Mmm… this is way too delicious."

So, he sat there, watching her eat her way through three-fourths of the pizza, taking small sips of coffee in between, tying him up in knots with the soft, mewling noises she made, seemingly unaware of them.

If this is how she relished her food, how would Princess react to a bout of hot sex with a passionate lover?

Rajvardhan swore as he got up suddenly, turning away abruptly to walk towards his bedroom. It was true that the milk would have made him go to sleep. But definitely not drinking it in the sexy Princess's company. Damn it all! It promised to be an extremely long night.

Chitrangada opened startled eyes when she heard him swear profusely, forgetting the coffee cup she was holding in her hand as she stared at Raj as he walked away. What was up with the man? He had been so cheerful and friendly but a few seconds ago. What had she done now? He was walking away without even wishing her 'good night'. Talk about being moody! She shrugged a slender shoulder, finishing her coffee.

Her stomach full and happy now, she was sure of sleeping well. And she did just that, the moment her head touched her pillow, not really bothered now about the lack of length in the sofa.

Rajvardhan tossed and turned on his bed, unable to sleep, not with the memory of the lovely woman sleeping not so far from him. It had all been a mistake — stopping to pick her up from the middle of the road, bringing her along with him to his hotel and letting her share his suite. What was the worst that could have happened if he hadn't stopped to help her? She would have gone back to her hotel room, where she belonged. But no, Prince Rajvardhan Thakore was not from an Indian royal family for nothing. He couldn't pass up an opportunity to help someone in distress, be it a man, woman or child. That is how he was wired.

But never before had someone he had rescued, managed to tie him in knots, not like the way Princess had. This just would not do. He so needed to rest before he took up practice for the upcoming polo match. He was to report at St Moritz three days from now, along with his team by evening, as they were taking part in the international snow polo event in the city that had been planned over the long weekend, a week later.

It was past six before oblivion claimed Rajvardhan's tired body and mind, completely unaware that the snow fall had taken over this part of Switzerland and had made the roads as well as railroads impassable. It looked like providence was playing a game with Raj and Princess, insisting on keeping them cloistered in the hotel suite for longer than either of them had planned.

3

aja Harischandra Gajanan held the glass of premium Scotch against the sunlight pouring through the windows of his breakfast parlour at his palace in Indore, Madhya Pradesh. The forty-eight-year-old belonged to the royal lineage of Gajanans who had ruled the eight-hundred-acre kingdom for two centuries from 1745 to 1950, before monarchy was declared obsolete in India.

Harischandra was one of those royals who had managed to retain a huge balance in his bank accounts, being a smart investor. He was five feet, eleven inches tall; lean, with well-developed muscles and was as healthy as a horse at his middle age. His farms flourished, though one couldn't say the same about his farmers since the Raja was quite stingy with his wealth.

He had been thirty when his parents had got him married to the princess of Gujarat. He had divorced Sitara two years later, making his parents terribly unhappy. His reason was that she couldn't produce the heir he craved. While Sitara had undergone a battery of tests that was proof enough that there was no reason why she couldn't conceive, Harischandra himself refused to have the doctors conduct tests on him as he *knew* that he was in perfect health, only because he had inherited his forefathers' genes that ensured he was totally virile. Sitara had been a couple of months over eighteen at that time—yes, their marriage had taken place when she had been but sixteen—and had made no protest, quietly going back to live with her parents, accepting the pittance that he gave her as one-time alimony settlement.

He had been thirty-seven when he set eyes on Akila, a dancing girl. The slim beauty had made him go crazy with longing, making him crave to make her his exclusive property. She had been elusive, too fond of her freedom and the money she made as a dancer. She also had had the liberty to pick and choose her lovers.

Harischandra had been relentless in his pursuit of her, not giving up as he visited the bar night after night, throwing money at her dainty feet, biding his time until she buckled under his attention.

A triumphant Harischandra married her eight months after the first time he saw her, excited to own her. But sadly, the cheerful and buoyant Akila began to fade away in the golden cage that her husband set up for her. She had everything wealth could buy her—clothes, jewellery, cars, luxurious trips across the globe, parties and what not. But she didn't have the one thing that she pined for—the freedom to do what she pleased. She was constantly at her husband's beck and call. She couldn't go out anywhere unless he accompanied her.

Harischandra didn't want his wife out of his sight. There were times when he travelled, times when she couldn't go along with him; those times he made sure that she didn't step out of the palace gates even for a walk.

It was a wonder that Akila had lasted for three years under the circumstances. Her beauty and effervescence seemed to fade right in front of his eyes, though it never struck Harischandra that he might be the cause for it. She became a shadow of the woman he had met the first time. She had stopped dancing and refused to listen to music, her heart breaking every time she heard a tune that called out to her.

Rumours flew around when Akila Gajanan fell to her death from the third-floor terrace of their palace after three years of marriage to Raja Harischandra Gajanan, at just twenty-nine. She had fallen on the rocks that were behind the palace and her body was found in bits and pieces. Had she committed suicide? Or had something more sinister happened to her? No one seemed to know. And there was none who was close enough to the Raja to ask him directly. The rest of them didn't even want to try as they weren't keen to drag the Raja's wrath on their heads. He could be vicious when he chose.

And yes, Harischandra could be as violent as he pleased, his pleasant and handsome countenance laying lie to the ruthless fiend that he actually was.

He was in a happy mood today, the whole of this week, in fact. The reason was Chitrangada Vasudeva, the princess of Jodhana.

He smacked his lips when he recalled her exquisite beauty. The princess was tall and slender, with luscious curves that made him drool. He had undressed her with his steely grey eyes as he devoured her beauty from the far end of the ballroom where he had been standing, eyeing her as she danced with one young man after the other. It was during a party at a common friend's palace in Gwalior.

He had liked it even more, the way she held herself, a bit aloof from every man she came in contact with. The filly was so obviously unbroken. That is when Raja Harischandra Gajanan had decided that Princess Chitrangada Vasudeva would become his third wife.

He had walked forward, his strides firm, before he tapped her dancing partner on his shoulder. The young man stopped mid-step, obviously startled, to turn and gaze at the Raja wildly.

"May I?" Harischandra adroitly pulled Chitrangada into his arms, before continuing the dance. He ignored the younger man, speaking to the princess, "Hello, Princess Chitrangada. Let me introduce myself. I'm Raja Harischandra Gajanan of Indore. How do you do?" He ignored the distaste on her lovely face, despite the effort she put in to hide it.

He wasn't really bothered as he was confident that she would come around once she got to know him better.

Princess Chitrangada had tilted her head back by a fraction of an inch, her stance royal to the core, all expression wiped out from her face now, except for the devil-may-care look in her eyes. "Raja or not, that was rude of you. Is that how you treat the people around you?"

His grey eyes gleamed, with temper as well as lust. He liked his women to be fighters. After all, what was the fun if they were all tame?! Chitrangada promised to be a tigress in bed, he concluded. "Then I must apologise. My only excuse is that I find you irresistible."

She rolled her eyes towards the ceiling before eyeing him with contempt, making his body thrum with excitement. "Shouldn't you be apologising to Samarth, instead of to me?"

Harischandra shrugged, turning her around in a circle, careful to hold her at arm's length, not wanting her to become privy to his arousal. "You are right," he sighed. "I'll do just that the moment the music stops."

Chitrangada smiled then, making the Raja only more determined to make her his. Her face was radiant, brighter than the sun at noon. He had to make her his or he might have to kill her. *But I definitely won't let you belong to anyone else;* he swore to himself.

The same night, after that dance, Harischandra left her alone, using his charm to befriend her father, Raja

Bikram Vasudeva of Jodhana, who was just forty-nine and closer in age to Harischandra, than his daughter, whom he coveted.

"I'm so happy to make your acquaintance, Raja Bikram Vasudeva. I've heard a lot about you," Harischandra lied through his teeth, "and have always wanted to meet you." He was charm personified as he stood next to Chitrangada's father, after they had toasted her beauty with premium Scotch whiskey.

Bikram was visibly excited. He had in truth heard a lot about Harischandra Gajanan and his infamous wealth. He felt envious as he eyed the other man who was just a year younger to him. "The pleasure is all mine, your highness. I have heard a lot about you too and I am mighty thrilled to meet you in person, finally." Though both were from royal households, they rarely moved in the same circles. "I heard that you travel eight months of the year and spend more time in Europe and South Africa than in India."

Harischandra didn't fail to catch the envy in the other man's voice. Unfortunately, he couldn't exactly recall much about Chitrangada's father or his fortunes. But he planned to find out every single detail about the father-daughter duo. Yes, he had got to know today that Bikram's wife had died when Chitrangada had been but a baby. It was just the two of them. If he needed to make the princess his, it was a smart move to become friendly with her father, who was more his contemporary.

He laughed now. "I plead guilty. It's just that I have varied businesses in those countries. You must know that I deal in precious gems, which yields about a tenth of my total revenue. And then…" He spoke in detail about his multiple business interests, watching with amusement at the way Bikram's mouth opened wider and wider.

It took Bikram two weeks and a lot of courage before he approached his new friend and asked for a loan of one crore. It was during the weekend that he had gone to spend at Harischandra's palace on the latter's invitation.

"My lands have failed and I'm into a lot of debt. If I don't pay off my creditors soon, it might be difficult to get my only child married off into a decent family." Bikram raised a hand, stopping Harischandra from interrupting as he continued, "My loans stand at only seventy lakhs. I plan to use the rest of the money to make the right investments before I return your money, with interest."

Harischandra didn't let on that he knew how Bikram Vasudeva had ended up with huge debts. The man was a gambler, cards being his major weakness. Worse than that, he was hopeless at the game. Considering that he was heading a royal household, he had next to no lands to his name, at least, not a great deal to speak of. Bikram had inherited five hundred acres of land and had been forced to sell four hundred of them to pay off his losses. He was still holding on to the last hundred acres only because his daughter had threatened to walk out of their home if he tried to sell them.

Yes, Harischandra had garnered a lot of information about Raja Bikram Vasudeva and his weaknesses in the past two weeks. One more thing he had found out was that while Bikram loved his daughter in his own way, he was absolutely selfish and his interests always came first, before anything else.

So, he was confident that with the right bait, he could easily convince Bikram to agree to Chitrangada's wedding with Harischandra.

Lending the man one crore was no big deal for Harischandra. Then, there was the one hundred acres of land that Bikram still owned. That would more than make for an ideal collateral, considering that the land value would be at least twelve crore rupees in the open market.

But he wanted to make Bikram stew. Let him wonder if Harischandra would help him. Only then would it be possible to convince him to give his daughter's hand to Harischandra. For the wily Raja of Indore hadn't forgotten that for all his looks and riches, Bikram might find him too old to be his daughter's bridegroom.

The cat and mouse game had continued over the next few months, Harischandra gaining ground as Bikram's desperation grew. His creditors were making threats nowadays.

And then Harischandra struck, just as would a cobra at its morbidly fascinated prey. "I have been thinking, Bikram, a lot. I have pots of money, but no heir to pass my wealth to. And you are impoverished, in need of money."

Bikram nodded vigorously, willing the other man to get to the point. Will Harischandra lend him the money or not? He was ready to accept anything the other man gave by now; any amount would do to shut up the hungry crocodiles.

"But you also have something that I want, something that is invaluable. Something one cannot attach a monetary value to. Something that I would give an arm and a leg to acquire."

Bikram Vasudeva stared at the other man, his jaw dropping open. What was the other man talking about? Could he mean his family heirlooms? Bikram had managed to salvage most of the jewellery collected by his forefathers. But why would Harischandra want those? If he had heard right, they were nowhere near as valuable as the tremendous collection Gajanan had.

Is the man a complete idiot or what? thought Harischandra, keeping the frown away from his face with great effort. "Come on Bikram, I don't have to spell it out to you."

Bikram shook his head in a daze, his mind still on his debts that were accruing interest by the lakhs, unable to concentrate on Harischandra's words. "It looks like you might have to, Harry. I'm unable to understand what you mean. You can't want my jewellery since they are nothing compared to your family heirlooms…" He stopped when he saw the other man shaking his head slowly.

"Let me be blunt. I've fallen for your daughter's beauty. I think she would make a perfect wife for me and give me the heir that I've been craving over the years." Harischandra's face had turned expressionless as he studied the other man with keen eyes.

"Huh!" Bikram Vasudeva paled as he stared at the other man in shock. "I… I don't get it, Harry. Why would you want to marry Chitrangada? She's too young for you." Could he be hearing right? If Harischandra meant what he said, then Bikram would never ever have an issue with money. The frown disappeared from his forehead as a slow smile spread across his swarthy face. "Er… what I mean is, are you sure? Chitrangada…"

"I have never been surer of anything in my life, Bikram." Excitement coated Harischandra's voice as he realised that he was very close to achieving his goal.

"It's just that Chitrangada is young enough to be your daughter. Will you be able to manage her?" The frown appeared again on Bikram's face, one that vied with the eagerness in his eyes, that Harischandra didn't fail to notice.

Harischandra laughed. "She's young, I agree. And she's *your* daughter, but not mine. I can see that you are worried that I might be too old for her. But you need not, you know. Many young ladies can vouch for my prowess in bed. Your daughter will have nothing to complain about." He removed a cigar from a silver case with great deliberation, before offering the box to Bikram.

Bikram laughed knowingly as he took a cigar and waited for the other man to light it, pleased to hear Harischandra join in the laughter. He sat back on the sofa, completely relaxed now as he puffed on the cigar. If Harischandra wanted his daughter for his wife, then he might as well ask for a few more crores than the measly one crore that he had been begging him for. And there will not be a question of even returning the money. It looked like the Gods were smiling at him just now. Wasn't he the lucky one! His daughter Chitrangada had turned out to be the personification of Goddess Lakshmi it seemed.

So, the two Rajas reached an agreement, neither of them feeling the need to consult the woman involved. After all, the patriarchs knew best, didn't they?! It was concluded that Raja Harischandra Gajanan of Indore would pay a dowry of five crore rupees to Raja Bikram Vasudeva of Jodhana to marry the latter's daughter.

Harischandra had grinned at his father-in-law-to-be, raising his glass in a toast. "You just forget that you ever had debts, Bikram. I'll take care of you and your daughter and that's a promise."

Coming back to the present, Harischandra smacked his lips as he recalled Chitrangada's lovely face and luscious figure. He couldn't wait to make her his. But he allowed Bikram to do things at his pace.

The engagement was to take place two months from now.

Phew!

It didn't matter. Harischandra also needed time to bring an end to his varied affairs. He planned to concentrate only on his wife and to make her pregnant with his heir as soon as possible.

He tilted his head back to toss the Scotch down his throat, happy with the way his life was unfolding just now.

hitrangada opened her eyes, pressing a dainty hand over her mouth as a yawn overtook her. She came wide awake though it was still dark. She turned her head towards the window where the curtains had been pushed aside by Raj the earlier night. A small scowl brought her eyebrows together. She felt so well rested while it had been past three in the morning when she finally went to sleep. How come it was still dark?

She got up to walk to the window and looked out, her eyes going wide when she saw the thick carpet of brilliant white snow covering every surface as far as she could see. And it was still snowing. "Brr!" She tucked her arms around herself, even if she felt toast warm inside the suite. It had obviously snowed throughout the night.

She finally located an electronic clock near the switchboard in the bedroom. Her jaw dropped in surprise when she noticed that it was eleven o'clock. But it seemed as if it was still early morning. She turned away abruptly when she caught the slight movement on the bed. Raj was stirring and she didn't want to be found standing next to him even if she was only checking the time. She swiftly walked to the bathroom and shut the door, not thinking to lock it.

Chitrangada stared at her flushed face in the mirror. Her hair was all over her face while Raj's t-shirt had slipped off one shoulder. She struck a model's pose in front of the mirror, smiling at her reflection, before giving a wink. There seemed to be a high possibility that she was going to be stuck in the hotel room as the snow didn't show any signs of abating. Her heartbeat picked up when she thought of the sexy Raj who was to be her roommate for at least one more day. Life promised to be fun! Even more so when she thought of how she had hoodwinked her bodyguards and consequently her father.

Her smile disappeared when she thought of what her father had done to her. He had promised her hand to Raja Harischandra who was all of twenty-three years her senior. They were to be engaged by the end of next month. Chitrangada had cajoled, argued, fought, threw tantrums, gone hungry for three days and more. But nothing had budged her father from his goal.

"Come on, Chitra, can't you do this much for your father's sake? I have brought you up singlehanded since your mother passed away. You were barely two then. But I didn't want you to suffer at some wicked stepmother's hands and solely took on the responsibility of bringing you up. Shouldn't you feel some kind of gratitude for that alone?" It was emotional blackmail at its worst.

"But, Dad, there must be some way that our financial problems could be resolved. I have a well-paying job and you very well know that." Chitrangada was an expert at restoring heritage buildings. She took up contracts with companies and made a tidy income as she worked hard and was really good at what she did along with a select team of likeminded people. "We'll surely get out of our financial troubles soon."

Bikram had shaken his head, refusing to meet Chitrangada's eyes. She had no clue that he owed seventy lakhs in gambling debts. He knew for a fact that his daughter—the one who was a gold mine right now—would just up and leave if she got to know that he had acquired such huge debts due to his gambling. And he didn't divulge to her that her prospective bridegroom was paying him five crores as dowry for her hand. "No, my dear. That's nowhere near enough. And your dad isn't growing younger. I so wish I could live a life of leisure after all these years of hard work." He moaned, slyly eyeing her face for reaction from the corner of his eyes.

"Dad, if you are old, what does that make Harischandra?" Chitrangada's black eyes sparked with fury as she glared at her father.

Bikram lifted his hands to bury his face in them. "Go away, you ungrateful child! I don't want to talk to you anymore. You do what you please. Why do you care what happens to your old father? You lead a happy life."

Chitrangada sighed. Now that was an argument to end all arguments. She was being ungrateful to begin with and now she was selfish. Talk about getting the raw end of the deal! She stopped arguing as she had an upcoming trip to Europe on work. What she hadn't expected was for her father to hire four well-muscled thugs to travel along with her.

"But Dad, why do I need bodyguards? I've always travelled on my own and there's never been a problem."

"That was before. Now that you're going to be Harischandra's bride, you need them for your safety. He's a billionaire, you know."

Chitrangada had gritted her teeth, continuing to glare at him. She stopped herself from saying anything as she realised that she would be wasting her breath.

Now she grinned at her reflection in the mirror. She still had three days to go before reporting for work. The idea to escape her bodyguards had been working on her mind all the way during the flight from India. And she had done just that at the first opportunity. She only wished that she hadn't forgotten to tuck her passport into her clutch.

Bikram Vasudeva wore a hole in the carpet as he paced up and down the hall at his palace. It was 11 pm in India. The head of his daughter's bodyguards,

Sharath, had called him at two in the afternoon and informed him that Chitrangada had run away. This was a circumstance that he had never expected. It had been nine hours since then. Where could she have gone in the middle of the night? And Sharath had mentioned that it had been snowing heavily, without a break. They had searched high and low for a couple of hours and had given up as the visibility was too bad. What Sharath hadn't admitted was that they hadn't bothered too much, presuming that the princess will have to get back to her room at the hotel before the night was over. After all, there wasn't much that a young woman could do on foot in the middle of the night, while it was snowing heavily in a strange country. They had begun to panic when she hadn't returned to her room at Hotel Storchen by 2 am. And that is when they decided to call her father in India.

"Idiots!" Bikram roared as he took an about turn before continuing his restless pacing. "Four of them and they couldn't keep track of one slip of a girl." Should he call the Indian consul in Zurich? Or should he wait for a while? One thing he was confident of. Nothing would have happened to harm his daughter. Chitrangada was too smart for one thing. And she was a karate blue belt for another. His main worry rose from the fact that she had deliberately run away, also the reason why he had hired the bodyguards in the first place.

Had that been a mistake? She probably wouldn't have felt the need to escape if they hadn't been around.

But then, she hadn't yet agreed to marry her beau and that was what was eating into Bikram's mind. If she refused to marry him, Raja Harischandra would kill Bikram for sure. Bikram had already received one crore from the other man and paid off his debts, playing around with the balance money, gambling more furiously than ever. And why not? He was going to receive two crores when the engagement happened and two more crores when the wedding took place. He could definitely afford to try his luck at cards, the recreation that he loved most.

Bikram decided to give it one more day before pressing the panic button and calling the consul. In the meanwhile, he had fired the bodyguards and told them to return to India immediately since their company was charging him round the clock for their services. Why pay good money to useless guys who couldn't do their jobs properly?

Rajvardhan came awake to the smell of her perfume—something citrusy and unique to Princess. He opened his eyes a slit and was startled to find the room empty. He was sure that she had been in his bedroom but a few moments ago. It was her proximity that had woken him up from a deep sleep.

Giving a mental shrug, he got up and walked to the bathroom to relieve himself, whistling under his breath. A muffled scream and a string of oaths made him turn his head to his right to notice that the shower curtains were closed and then heard the shower itself. Shit! Princess was in the bath. Realising that he was buck naked, he pulled a bath sheet from the railing and wrapped himself in it.

"No worries, Princess. You're safe. Good morning, by the way." His voice shook with laughter, as his heart soared, glad to know that she hadn't been a figment of his imagination.

"Will you get out of the bathroom?" Chitrangada's voice was strangled as she shut the shower. Goose bumps ran all over her body as she glared at the shower curtain which was the only thing that came between the two of them.

"Hmm. Did I hear you say 'please'"? Rajvardhan, who had been on his way out, stopped right where he was to ask her the question, thoroughly amused by the situation. He decided to ignore his aroused body. No way was he going to acknowledge it.

"Are you crazy, Raj? How dare you walk into the bathroom when I'm in the shower?" Chitrangada's hands were tightly fisted now as she stamped her foot in the marble bath. All the towels were on the other side of the shower curtain and she was beginning to feel cold now.

"But, your highness, you must forgive me." Rajvardhan was openly laughing now as he walked towards the bath. "The bathroom door was not locked and I had forgotten that I was sharing the suite with a princess, no less."

"Keep away from me." Chitrangada lifted her arms to cross them over her breasts, wariness in her gaze as she could see his shadow moving closer through the semi-opaque curtains.

"With pleasure," he said, taking another bath sheet and throwing it over the curtain rail. "There you are. I'll see you outside." He did an about turn and walked out of the bathroom, having teased her enough.

Chitrangada managed to catch the bath sheet in both her arms and wrapped it around her from neck to calf. Raj managed to confound her, every time. She had obviously been wrong in thinking that he would attack her modesty. Should she apologise to him for that? Maybe she will. She towelled herself dry before wrapping a bathrobe around her slender body. She checked to see that the hem touched her knees. Decent enough!

She knocked on the bathroom door just in case he was loitering in the bedroom with not a stitch on. Not hearing any sound, she pushed the door an inch to peep outside. Seeing that the bedroom was empty, she stepped out with a sigh, before walking into the sitting room, her eyes zeroing in on her tormentor who was standing at the window, gazing outside.

Hearing her behind him, Rajvardhan said without turning, "It looks like we are stuck with each other for at least another day."

"Do you think so?" She didn't let on that she had arrived at the same conclusion earlier. "Should we call the reception to find out?"

"I just did." He turned towards her, clad in the shorts from the earlier night, only this time he had also thrown a t-shirt over his upper body, covering that magnificent chest. "Aah! You might need more clothes. Isn't it a good thing that I'm carrying lots of those."

She sniffed, lifting her chin in the air and glaring at him. "I'm sure the hotel boutique must have something. Let me go buy some."

"You plan to go shopping in that bathrobe? I have no issues. But the hotel management might not approve." He was grinning as he walked to the phone. "I'm hungry and plan to order a huge breakfast. Unless you would like to go down to the restaurant?"

"I thought the staff will disapprove of my running amok in their hotel in this bathrobe?" Chitrangada knew she had a hot temper, but she usually managed to keep it under wraps without too much effort. But Raj seemed to bring out the worst in her. Anger had been the uppermost emotion that she had been feeling since the moment she met him.

He turned to look at her, running his coffee brown gaze from the top of her head to the tips of her painted toes. He didn't miss the casual knot of her long hair on the top of her crown, with unruly curls dancing around her flushed cheeks. With no makeup on, she looked barely twenty, her rosy lips parted, giving him a view of a perfect set of pearly whites. His gaze stopped for an extra few seconds on her luscious breasts which rose and fell as she took deep breaths, obviously working hard at holding on to her temper, before it moved down to take in her whole body. Delicious! That is what she was. He bunched his fists, controlling the urge to fold her in his arms and make leisurely love to her.

"Let us have breakfast here in the room. Then I'll go and buy some clothes for you at the said boutique. Does that find favour with your highness?" He asked, tongue firmly in cheek, his eyes twinkling with mischief.

Well, two could play at the game. She sat down on a single sofa, crossing one leg over the other. "Works well for me." Unable to resist, she gave him a regal nod before shutting one eye in a sly wink.

Colour ran up Rajvardhan's rugged cheeks. At least another twenty-four hours in her company. Will he be able to keep his hands to himself? He hoped that his *kshatriya* blood from a long line of royals would give him the control that he so needed just now.

"Your order, ma'am?"

Refusing to be cowed, Chitrangada said, "Some French toast and coffee should do."

"Right." Rajvardhan turned his back on her, only because he didn't want her to notice the state of his arousal before placing her order and his own for a full English breakfast.

Once they were done with their respective meals, he almost ran out of the suite, to escape her proximity, even if only for the fifteen minutes it took him to complete her shopping. Oh, how he enjoyed purchasing some seriously sexy bras and panties, a pair of jeans, a couple of t-shirts, a dressy top and an evening dress for her. As for her size, well, Rajvardhan knew his women pretty well. He also threw in a hair brush, a pot of moisturiser, a compact, an eyeliner and a couple of tubes of lipsticks for good measure into the eager arms of the saleswoman.

"Here you go," he said, handing the shopping bags to Chitrangada on his return. "I hope you have all you need."

"Give me the bill. I'll return the money the moment I can." She rummaged through the bags and blushed hotly when she noticed the two matching sets of silk and lace bras and panties, in red and peach. What the hell! Raj was obviously an expert at buying clothes for women. Gritting her teeth, she looked him in the eye. "Okay?"

He shrugged. "If that's what you want, Princess."

"Yeah, I do." She walked swiftly into the bedroom and shut the door, tilting the contents of the bags on the unmade bed, checking out all the stuff that he had bought for her. Her cheeks continued to flame as she chucked the bathrobe before donning the peach lace. Not surprisingly, they fitted her to perfection. She couldn't face herself in the mirror as she quickly pulled on the stretch jeans which fit her snugly. Ignoring the temptation to wear the dressy top, she chose the white t-shirt that had the logo of the hotel printed on the back. Brushing her hair vigorously, she pulled it into a loose knot at the nape of her neck, before applying moisturiser and a nude gloss to her lips. It wasn't easy ignoring the painful arousal of her breasts and the sudden moisture between her legs as her mind drew pictures of Raj's hands on the lingerie.

She walked out to say, "Thank you, Raj. I feel much better."

He didn't reply as he ran his eyes over her once again, liking what he saw, only too much. He had obviously got her size exactly right. She wore a 32 C cup bra and small size panties. It was a shame that he wouldn't be helping her out of those. He simply nodded, unable to find his voice.

It promised to be the longest day of his life!

hen Rajvardhan and his team received the cup after coming first in the Snow Polo World Cup finals at St Moritz more than a week later, it didn't really excite him as much as he had expected it to. He had been participating in the snow polo event since the last two years and this was the first time his team had bagged first place. It was a truly high honour. But a pair of black-as-coal eyes and luscious pink lips kept intruding between him and everything else.

He wasn't really sure what he said in his acceptance speech and subsequent interviews with TV channels, newspapers, and online portals. But he obviously made sense since no one gave him odd looks.

He had been sequestered with Princess in his hotel suite for not one, but three days and nights. While they had been arguing most of their waking hours, they had also spent a lot of time at peace with one another. He had been carrying four books and they had done some reading too. They also played cards to while away the time. Neither of them much into watching TV, they had stuck to checking the news channels on and off to keep track of the weather. This was all during the first day after the night they had checked in.

Rajvardhan had wondered if someone was missing her. But she seemed fine without her phone or any contact with anyone—either family or friends. Not that she was keen to talk about either.

"So, what do you do, Princess? Other than being pretty?"

That had set her teeth on edge, much to his amusement. He couldn't resist rattling her chain at every opportunity!

Her right eyebrow had gone up haughtily at that. "What do you think a Princess does, Raj? I give orders, of course. And sit on a huge throne next to my father and sentence people to life imprisonment or even death in some cases. All this apart from the facials and manicures that I get done on a daily basis."

Rajvardhan laughed, catching the tempestuous gleam in her eyes. "Am I glad that I'm not one of your subjects!"

"Maybe not. But I'm seriously thinking of making you my slave," was her quick comeback.

Rajvardhan didn't admit how close she was to the truth as he was falling for her wit and beauty slowly but surely. He shook his head at her in reply. "That's naughty of you, Princess, and not really fair to me." He tried to put on a puppy dog look on his face but failed miserably.

It was Chitrangada's turn to laugh, drawing his gaze to the dimples on her cheeks. "So, what do you do, Raj? Other than globe-trotting?" She knew by now that he was from Udaipur, not all that far from where she lived.

"I run to the rescue of stranded women in foreign countries for one thing. As for the other, I am building a horse farm back home, mainly catering to polo ponies." He turned serious as he looked into her eyes while replying to her question.

"Ooh!" Her eyes had gone wide with excitement. "You have a horse farm. That's so awesome. How many horses do you have on it?"

"A dozen horses and five mares as of now. Planning to add more in the near future."

"And polo ponies?"

"Yeah, I'm training most of them to play polo."

"You are training them? Do you play?"

He smiled. Rajvardhan Thakore's name was synonymous with polo since the past seven years. But she was not to know that. "I do."

She opened up after that and told him a bit about her career of renovating heritage buildings and what she had come to Zurich to do.

He nodded his head several times, listening to her — not just her words, but her soft voice that strummed on the strings of his heart. When there was a lull in the conversation, he told her that he was taking part in the Snow Polo World Cup event at St Moritz.

"This is the third year since my team began to participate. Playing on snow is very different from playing on a grass field. But it's definitely an exhilarating experience."

Chitrangada nodded, not having much knowledge about the game. But there was admiration in her gaze.

"So, do you have a girlfriend?" She asked him, her black gaze looking with enquiry into his brown one. Such a handsome hunk must probably have a girlfriend in every city he visited.

Rajvardhan shook his head. "No, I don't. Never had a serious one. What about you, Princess? You must have had men chasing you since your teens, if not earlier." While he pretended to tease her, he meant it. She looked so beautiful. He could just imagine her as a leggy teenager, young men running behind her, vying for her attention.

Chitrangada laughed softly. "None that I was aware of. But yes, I've had a couple of crushes." Soft colour flared up her cheeks as she continued, "One when I was in junior college and another during my final year of graduation."

"So, what happened? You mean to say that neither man was good enough for your royal highness?"

She pouted at him, unaware of the effect she was having on him. "It looks like I wasn't good enough for either."

"Now that I find difficult to believe." It was Rajvardhan's turn to deal the cards and he did so without taking his eyes off her, a smile on his face. It seemed like he stood a chance now.

"And by the way, I'm getting engaged by the end of next month." There was no smile on her face when she said that. If she had her way, the marriage wouldn't take place, with or without the engagement ceremony. But she had wanted to tell Raj about it, only because she wanted to see his reaction.

Rajvardhan was shell shocked, to put it mildly. It was with great difficulty that he stopped his face from going completely stiff. But he couldn't do much when his smile disappeared and refused to come back. "Really! Congratulations, Princess. Who's the lucky man? Is it a love match?"

Not exactly the response she had expected from him. What was with the man? Cooped in a suite with an attractive woman, didn't he feel anything at all for her? How she wished that she could have a wild affair with him, if nothing else! But having never made love with anyone before, nor having felt the urge to do so, she didn't really know how to let Raj know what she wanted.

Chitrangada shook her head slowly from side to side, her gaze lowered to the table, refusing to meet the intense expression in his eyes. "My father has arranged my wedding to this man." She didn't want to take Harischandra Gajanan's name and make the situation more real than what it was, while she couldn't do much about her drooping lips as she still hadn't found a way out of the situation. Though she hadn't completely given up, either.

Rajvardhan felt compelled to change the subject and they spoke about his passion for horses which she seemed to share. There were two horses back home that Chitrangada rode whenever she found time which was fairly often as she simply adored the activity.

It was Chitrangada who was sleepless on the second night. How much ever she tried to find faults with Raj's behaviour, she found herself attracted to him. He could be charming when he chose to be and did have a strong chivalrous streak. She also realised that he lost his cool only when she tried his patience too hard.

They had decided to go to bed early, hoping that the snow would be cleared by morning and they could both go their separate ways.

The sofa that had seemed alright the earlier night, refused to yield any solace that night. She twisted and turned, the sheets bunching under her, only making her feel worse.

"Tch!" Chitrangada got up to sit on her makeshift bed. What the fuck! Why the hell was she suffering in the cramped space when there was a huge king-sized bed in the other room? Agreed that Raj was big built. But the bed was large enough to fit three men of his size. She got up from the sofa, determination on her face. She didn't care what he would have to say tomorrow, but she needed the comfort of a proper bed.

She carried the comforter along with her and slipped silently into the empty half of the bed Rajvardhan was lying on and went to sleep the moment her head touched the pillow.

Sometime later, in the throes of deep sleep, Rajvardhan turned on his side and snuggled into her warmth, throwing an arm around her soft body and pulling her close to his naked torso. Without realising what he was doing, he had pushed her comforter out of the way and shared his with her. Sighing deeply, he continued to sleep, a smile on his face as he dreamed of making love to Princess.

It was early morning when Chitrangada opened her eyes a slit, becoming aware of something heavy against her chest as well as her legs. Huh! Coming wide awake, her hand encountered a hairy forearm that was fit snugly against her chest. Hot colour burned her cheeks when she became aware of a large hand cupping her left breast. She reached a hand lower and found a muscular leg wrapped around both of hers. She couldn't see much from her position, her back pressed to his torso and with the comforter covering both of them. But, of course, she could make out that she was in the sleeping Raj's arms.

And whose fault was that! And if she wasn't mistaken, he didn't have a stitch of clothing on.

But before she could do something about the situation, she felt the warmth of his breath against her neck, goose bumps flaring all over her skin as her body responded with alacrity. Her breasts tingled even as the tips tightened, a deep sigh emanating from her as she felt his lips against the pulse on her neck.

"Princess…" Rajvardhan's voice was the softest of whispers as his hand tightened around her soft, luscious breast, even as he pulled her body closer to his. Not fully aware of what he was doing, he automatically pressed his lower body to hers, revelling in the fit of her lush bottom against his loins.

Chitrangada's eyes went wide when she felt his hard shaft against her butt. Oh my God! She rolled in his arms to face him, doing her best to put some space between them. What actually resulted was that she was crushed against his chest as he pulled her closer, her breasts coming into contact with his hard, muscular body. The thin t-shirt that she wore was too flimsy a barrier as her breasts rejoiced in the contact. The hand that she had put on his shoulder to push him away, had no strength left as she caressed his bronzed skin, her eyes studying the movement of her own hand in morbid fascination.

"Princess…" Rajvardhan buried his face in her shoulder, placing tender kisses along the slope, his breath coming in soft gasps. She looked lovely with her soft curls tumbling all over her shoulders and back, her dark eyes still smudged with sleep, though he couldn't miss the burgeoning desire peeping through them.

"Raj…" Chitrangada protested weakly, her body closing the small distance between them as it seemed to have a mind of its own as it refused to follow her order to stay away from the sinful temptation that was presented to her that morning.

She forgot her own name when he closed his lips over hers, catching the sound of his name as he kissed her. First softly, his mouth brushing light as a feather over her trembling lips. Then slowly, the tip of his tongue reaching out to trace the pouting shape. Then thoroughly as he drew her lower lip into his mouth, sucking on it slowly and deeply, making her moan with want. "Raj…"

"Do you like it, Princess?" He whispered against her lips, before his tongue plunged deep into the recesses of her mouth, making her mind go completely blank as a deep need coursed through her, a need that she had never experienced before, a need to become his, completely.

She threw her free arm around his neck to pull his head closer, allowing him complete access to her mouth as she tangled her tongue with his, revelling in the sensation. She also threw a long and slim leg over his waist, pressing her lower body close to his tumescent manhood, welcoming his hardness. "Oh, yes," she moaned, sucking on his tongue, making him groan with need.

Rajvardhan pushed at the t-shirt, his large hand moving restlessly over her small waist as it moved above, one inch at a time, before he cupped the underside of her bare breast, making her moan all the more. He raised a thumb to brush it over the engorged tip, moving his head away to smile down at her when he felt her nipple go hard. "I want to love you, all the way."

"What's stopping you, Raj?" Chitrangada pressed open-mouthed kisses to his rough cheek, rubbing a damp tongue wherever she could reach, mewling like a kitten. Caught in the deep throes of passion, she didn't care that he was an almost stranger. Nor did she care that she might never see him after today. Just now, she was exactly where she wanted to be, half naked in Raj's arms, being kissed wildly. She wanted all of him, even if it was going to be just this once.

Instead of encouraging him, her words seemed to make Rajvardhan wary. He came awake fully to move away from her marauding lips and stare at her intent face. "Are you sure, Princess? I…"

"Don't tell me you're developing cold feet at this very moment?" Chitrangada looked at him, her charcoal gaze challenging. "I can see that you want me."

More than any other woman in the world! Yes, Rajvardhan was totally aware that his body clamoured for its union with hers. But then, for all her boldness, he could see that Princess was an innocent. "Listen…"

She moved, pressing her body to his while closing her mouth over his, her left hand reaching out hesitantly to touch his manhood, gathering confidence as she felt him swell under her tentative caress. She kissed him awkwardly as it was the first time she had taken the lead. The couple of times that she had been kissed, she had never enjoyed the experience. But she so hungered for Raj's kisses. She had to concede that the man was an expert. She gave a soft sigh now when he took over to kiss her thoroughly.

Rajvardhan was only too glad to make love to her as his body screamed for hers. Her stumbling caresses of his manhood was driving him crazy with longing, her soft hand arousing him painfully. He pushed her gently down on the bed before lifting the t-shirt and pulling it off her body, his eyes devouring the twin globes that looked up at him invitingly. She was clad in a pair of bikini briefs that just about covered her femininity. He looked deeply into her eyes, saying, "You look gorgeous," and was satisfied when dark colour flared up her dimpling cheeks. He took both her hands in his and placed them at her sides, bending down to kiss her forehead. He then traced his lips over her fluttering eyelids and down her cheeks, not really surprised when he felt her hands on his back as she ran them feverishly over his skin, her legs moving restlessly. With a smile, he kissed the tip of her nose, saying, "Impatient, are we?"

Her eyes opened wide at his words. "Aren't you?" she challenged him provocatively.

Rajvardhan laughed softly. "Oh yeah, from the moment I set eyes on you." He bent down to kiss her on the lips again, his tongue exploring the contours lazily even as he felt her nails digging into his back, feeling the tremors in her body. He traced a path with his lips from her cheek to her ear, taking a nip before climbing down her neck to the shoulder, taking his own sweet time, whispering words of appreciation as he tasted and sucked. He stopped at the slope of her breast, lifting his head to stare down again at her lovely mounds, his eyes glowing with desire as he watched the peaks tighten under his gaze. He bent down to trace a damp tongue in a circular path around her left breast, his left-hand cupping her right breast. The circles grew tighter and tighter, as he got closer to the aureole.

Chitrangada's breath was stuck in her throat as she clutched his head in both her hands, pulling him closer even as she lifted her upper body to thrust it closer to his marauding mouth and hands, moaning with need as he took his own sweet and torturous time, making love to her. She moaned long and loud when his warm mouth finally closed over the hard tip of her left breast. She fell back on the bed, only aching for more when he suckled her deeply. "Raj…"

It was a long time before he lifted his head to blow gently over the wet tip of her breast, watching with satisfaction as it puckered. His mouth traced a path across her chest to give the same dedicated attention to her right breast, his right hand travelling southwards, over her abdomen, a lazy finger dipping into her navel before moving further down to caress the triangle that was still covered. He pulled her panties down her thighs, not taking his mouth off her breast. Chitrangada helped him along by shimmying out of the minuscule garment, gasping when she felt his warm hand caressing her most private part. "Yes…"

Rajvardhan moved her left leg, his hand a caress against her silken thigh, before placing a gentle finger at her entrance, grinning when he felt her almost jump off the bed. "Like it?" he asked, probing further.

"Too much, Raj. Don't stop."

"Don't plan to," he promised, delving deeper, satisfied to find her all wet and ready to receive him. "Is this your first time?"

"What if it is?" Chitrangada glared at him, her temper flaring as she grew defiant.

"Will you just chill, Princess?" He kissed her cheek in a gentle caress. "I'm just being careful not to hurt you here."

She turned her head to press her lips to his, apologising without uttering the words. "It is."

"A little bit of initial pain and you should be fine," He consoled.

"And how would you know?" Chitrangada's voice shook with sudden amusement. She felt so cherished.

Rajvardhan laughed outright. "Good question. Suffice to say that I know."

She reached out a hand to caress his throbbing shaft. If what she had heard was right, he must have phenomenal control. He had been hard even as she had woken up that morning. But he was so patient, overwhelming her with his gentle lovemaking. "Come, Raj. I want you inside me."

"With pleasure." Taking a condom out of his wallet that lay on the bedside table, he rolled it over himself and rose above her. He pulled her right leg around his waist. She responded immediately by throwing her other leg and locking her ankles behind him. Her arms encircled his neck in a stranglehold and her eyes were shut tightly, while she bit down hard on her lips. "Princess, are you in pain?"

She opened her eyes a slit to look at him, shaking her head slowly from side to side. "No…"

He smiled, a tender expression on his face. "Relax, sweetheart. I promise not to hurt you, at least not much."

Chitrangada tried to, only getting more tensed up in the process. Realising that he was going about it in the wrong way, Rajvardhan kissed her again, slowly but deeply, feeling her body language change from tension to passion. He caressed her sensitised breasts with his tongue even as his finger stroked her core. Finding her wet, he gently pushed the tip of his shaft into her, moving slowly but steadily, groaning with suppressed need. He pressed on against her barrier until it gave, swallowing her moan of pain as he placed his lips against the corner of mouth. "I'm sorry, sweetheart." He waited for her body to adjust to him and was rewarded when he felt her pelvic muscles relax before she moved closer to him in demand.

He pulled out of her, pleased to hear her moan of protest before pushing into her again. She didn't let him be gentle now as she became more demanding, her legs locked tightly around his lean waist while she pummelled his back with her small fists. "Raj... I want more."

And he pounded into her, relentlessly, forgetting himself in the pleasure that built within him, ready to explode even as he felt the tremors of her orgasm against his manhood.

Chitrangada fell back on the bed; her moans having turned to soft screams as she shook in the aftermath of the most earth shattering experience of her life. So, this is what sex was all about. Before she could recover from her first orgasm, she could feel another one building deep down within her as Raj continued to plumb into her depths. It wasn't long before they came together, groaning as one in satisfaction before Rajvardhan fell against her. She wouldn't let him move away even as he tried to.

"I might crush you with my weight," he said, holding her close, his face buried in her neck.

"I don't care, but don't you dare move away from me." She had the last word, her lips pressed to the top of his head, falling asleep in his arms almost immediately.

Wide awake, Rajvardhan turned his head around before finding a comfortable position against her plump breasts, closing his eyes with a sigh, a satisfied smile on his face. That had been a mind-blowing experience indeed. For a novice, Princess had been amazing in bed, more than compensating with her enthusiasm. He almost laughed out loud when he thought of the way she tried to manoeuvre him, demanding into the bargain. He held her for a long time, not having the heart to leave alone the sleeping woman in his arms.

It was more than an hour before Chitrangada woke up, stretching luxuriously, revelling in the unfamiliar aches and pains that had taken over her body that still felt tender from Raj's lovemaking. She smiled, recalling and relishing every detail as she inadvertently caressed his silky head that lay against her breasts, enjoying the heaviness on her chest. Raj was not just handsome and well-mannered, he was a terrific lover too. Colour ran up her cheeks as she continued to ruminate over the morning, glad that she had taken the decision to sleep in his bed. She couldn't help wondering if he would have taken the initiative to make love to her if she hadn't landed up in his arms the way she had. Raj had as good as admitted to wanting her from the moment he set eyes on her. She blushed some more on thinking that, her body throbbing with desire when she felt him come awake, even before his mouth closed over a turgid nipple. "Raj…" she moaned, "that feels so good."

He suckled and stroked both her breasts, going about it gently as he realised that she was probably sore. He turned on his back and pulled her above him, placing a soft kiss on her lips. "How are you?"

Her dark eyes gleamed with excitement and desire. "Ne'er been better," she declared vehemently. "How about you?"

Rajvardhan laughed, his hands caressing her bottom. "Ditto," he said, "You were simply amazing."

"I can do better. Wanna find out?" She wiggled her eyebrows at him, her arms folded and tucked under her chin as she lay on his chest. His hard body felt so good under her soft one.

Rajvardhan laughed again. "Would love to, but maybe later at night. I…"

She rolled off him to sit up, her legs on the floor, ready to run away. "I can take a straightforward 'no', you know." Her cheeks were flaming in mortification. Why the hell had she asked him? But then, was it only the prerogative of a male to wish for sex? If that is what Raj believed, then he wasn't what she had thought he was.

Grasping immediately that he had offended her without meaning to, he got up too, grabbing her hand and pressing it against his engorged manhood. "Does that seem like a 'no'?" he asked, his lips brushing against her ear, even as a gentle hand shifted her hair out of the way. "I meant it when I said that I wanted to make love to you from the moment I set eyes on you. And that hasn't changed one little bit." He pulled her on his lap, her back against his chest, his hands cupping her breasts. "I'm unable to keep my hands off you, as you can see for yourself."

She held his forearms, staring down at his bronzed hands against her pale skin, her head falling back against his shoulder, eyes closing of their own volition. "Then why?" Chitrangada moaned.

"You, my sweetheart, must be sore. I just want to give you time to heal."

Chitrangada looked into his eyes and seeing the banked passion under the gentleness, fell headlong in love with him.

They made love again that night, Rajvardhan teaching her how to please him while he explored all her erogenous zones. They weren't too bothered when they found out the next morning that they were going to be snowed in for at least one more day, spending the whole day in bed, ordering room service.

Chitrangada woke up on the fourth day, wrapping a towelling robe around her body as she looked down at the sleeping Raj. He was lying on his chest, the comforter covering the lower half of his body. She bent down to caress the golden skin of his back and stopped herself just in time. It was time to go. A call to the reception had confirmed that the roads were fit to travel in.

She heaved a sigh. These three days had been a slice of heaven, but it was time to face reality. She had better get back to her hotel room. She needed to talk to her father before getting on with the work she had come to Zurich for.

Raj! Well, it had been wonderful making love with him. But at no point had he mentioned anything about a permanent commitment or even a relationship. He was extremely handsome and a man of the world. For all she knew, she could have been a temporary distraction.

Chitrangada came to a decision. She wasn't going to hang around, waiting for him to dismiss her. She swiftly and silently packed all her new clothes that he had bought her—she would treasure them for life—into a haversack and threw in the t-shirt that he had given her to use as nightwear. Donning her jeans and t-shirt, she left the suite, closing the door silently behind her.

Rajvardhan woke up more than an hour later, his mouth upturned in a smile as he reached out for his lover. He opened his eyes when he encountered the empty bed. Looking at the clock, he saw it was past ten in the morning. She must be in the bathroom. He whistled as he walked over. It was time to make love in the shower.

Finding the bathroom door open, he grinned to himself, calling out even as he stepped in, "Are you in the shower, sweetheart?"

The shower curtains were open and there was no Princess to greet him. Rajvardhan walked out quickly and into the sitting room. Where was she? Had she gone down to the reception?

He would go down too and maybe they could have breakfast in the restaurant. He walked to the window and was pleased to see that the snow had stopped and the road had been cleared. Good!

He went back to the bedroom and opened the wardrobe to remove his jeans and shirt. That was when he noticed that Princess's clothes were missing.

What the fuck!

Fifteen minutes later, after going through the whole suite looking for a note from her, Rajvardhan realised that Princess had walked out of his life, without a way for him to find her.

I don't care! Rajvardhan told himself again and again. The more number of times he uttered the words like a slogan, the deeper he was convinced of the lack of truth in them.

Maybe she had taken his number from the hotel staff. Maybe she would call him soon. Rajvardhan's wait was in total vain.

Had Princess been using him? To break the monotony for one thing. Or maybe she had been trying to gain some experience before getting engaged and later married to whoever the hell that was. But then, she hadn't been happy about her upcoming engagement, even presuming that she had been telling him the truth. Oh yes, Princess had fed him a number of lies. But her body hadn't lied. She had craved him as much as he desired her, even now. Just two nights and one day of lovemaking was nowhere near enough.

He needed a whole lifetime with her. That is when Rajvardhan came to a decision.

He would find Princess, whichever corner of the earth she had disappeared to and even if it was the last thing he did. He didn't give a damn about the man she was going to be betrothed to. He would pull her out of the jaws of death, if need be, to make her his.

6

Her father was furious when Chitrangada called him on that Thursday after she had returned to her room in Hotel Storchen.

"This is the ultimate, Chitra. How dare you…?"

"Dad! Before you say something you might come to regret, please understand that I was stranded. You must know that there was a blizzard here and nothing moved over the past three days. And…"

"But you should have been in your hotel room at that point, with those bodyguards to keep you safe. Only, you decided to run away when there was absolutely no need to. Did you even think of how worried I must have been?" He was shouting again.

"Come on, Dad. You know better than to be worried about me. What do you think could have happened? I booked myself into another hotel for the night. It's just that I couldn't get away from there since the whole country had come to a standstill. Now that I am back in my room, the first thing I'm doing is to call you. There's no need for you to be upset."

"All very well for you to say," muttered Bikram. He grumbled on for some more time until Chitrangada pleaded that she had meetings to reschedule since she had wasted three days already. "And thanks for getting those goons off my back," she said, a smile in her voice. There had been a message on her phone that the bodyguards' services had been terminated. That had been from their company.

"Waste of money, that's what they were," said Bikram angrily.

"I told you so in the first place." His cheeky daughter blew him a kiss after that parting shot before cutting the line.

Her mind insisted on flying back to Raj and the glorious time she had spent with him. Her body ached for his touch while her breasts throbbed with need. Her womb screamed silently for him. But she determinedly ignored everything as she threw herself into work and crammed as much as she could, to avoid thoughts of him. But she couldn't do anything during the night. She stayed awake into the wee hours, tossing on her bed, thinking about him.

But Chitrangada was made of sterner stuff. Yes, she had had her fun with Raj. She had better accept that it had been temporary. Wasn't she wiser now? She had experienced hot, steamy sex. She tried to smile at her reflection in the mirror, but her face felt stiff. Time! That is what she needed, to forget Raj.

She went back home ten days later. It was evening when she got out of the car which had picked her up at Udaipur airport a couple of hours ago. "Dad!" She hugged her father on entering their palace. "How have you been?"

Bikram was extremely cheerful, what with his creditors off his back and the extra thirty lakh rupees which he could use however he pleased. In his case, it meant that he had a lot of funds for gambling. He had been careful with the cash while a sudden winning streak had kept him enthralled over the past week. He had stopped being angry with his daughter and had not given much thought about her protests when he had spoken to her about her betrothal to Raja Harischandra Gajanan.

They had dinner together and even went for a walk. They both were close to each other that way. It was only as she grew older that Chitrangada had taken to arguing with him regarding almost everything.

Bikram bided his time over the next couple of days and opened the subject on Saturday morning at the breakfast table. "So, Chitra, I was thinking that March 30, being a Friday, will be perfect for your betrothal. What do you say?"

Chitrangada kept her cloth napkin aside before sitting back straight in her chair, her black eyes studying her father intensely. He had obviously not given up on the idea, yet. "Dad, you very well know what I think of this idea of yours. I don't like Raja Harischandra. For one thing, he's too old for me and for another, he gives me the creeps."

"Don't be silly, Chitra. Harry is a gentleman and a true royal, I must say. Over and above all that, he's a billionaire and believe me, that can definitely make life easier for all of us. I agree with you that he's a little bit older than you…"

"Little bit?" Chitrangada got up, pushing her chair back noisily, obviously agitated. "Dad, he's twenty-three years my senior, close to your age actually. I can't envisage…"

"Sit down, Chitra and stop shouting." Bikram's voice was firm as he ordered her. "As I was saying, Harry is older than you, but I can only say that it's all the better for you. You are mature and sophisticated. Can you think of one young man who can match up with you?" There was triumph in his voice as he looked at his daughter, pride in his eyes as to the wonderful young woman that she had grown up to be.

A handsome face with slashed cheeks and a mischievous smile in melting chocolate eyes flashed before her mind's eye. Raj would have been perfect for her. Have been? He *was* the man she would choose, if the choice was hers. But, Chitrangada sighed, in the beginning, he had not been moved when she had mentioned that she was going to be engaged soon. Later, after they had made love, he had not said anything about having feelings for her. If he had been interested in her emotionally, even one small percentage of what she felt for him, he would have said something, wouldn't he?

Damn it all! Why was life so complicated? She did not remember her mother who had died when she was barely two. It had been only her father and herself.

She had been happy, until the time when she had met Yashodhara Singh Jadeja in kindergarten. Her life had only got better after that. The two little girls had hit it off immediately, even though Yashodhara had been almost a year older. They became fast friends and had spent as much time together as was possible.

Until one fine day, when they had been in Std VII, Yasho had stopped coming to school. An anxious Chitrangada had called her best friend's home only to speak to her mother. Yashodhara had fallen ill with a severe form of chicken pox. Chitrangada had waited forever for her friend to return to school after her recovery. But no such luck. Yashodhara had disappeared from her life.

Chitrangada couldn't get too close to anyone after that. Of course, she had many 'friends', but no one she could call a best friend. Just now, she wished there was someone she could talk to, someone who would tell her what to do. She did not want to upset her father, but he was asking her for the impossible. Why should she marry someone she could not imagine even liking?

"Dad, please try to understand my point of view. Marriage is for keeps as you very well know. Even you couldn't marry a second time after Mom passed on." Chitrangada believed in the fairy tale that her father had spun to her about his marriage to her mother. What he never told his daughter was that he had not liked the idea of being shackled to one woman and though he had missed his wife in his own way after her death, he could not face the prospect of being tied to another woman, not in this lifetime.

Just now Bikram stared at his daughter. He did not want to tell her about the monetary deal that he had struck with Raja Harischandra Gajanan. She would hate him if she ever got to know about it. The money had not only helped him pay off his debts, it had boosted his confidence in a long way. If he had had a son, wouldn't the boy have earned money and taken care of his father? Chitrangada spoke so much about gender equality. Why shouldn't she take charge of her father's finances in this way?

But deep down, Bikram knew that Chitrangada would be furious if she got to know about the five-crore dowry that Harischandra had promised for her hand. How could he persuade her to agree to the wedding without letting her know the full truth?

"Look here, Chitra. This wedding will make your old father happy. If that counts for something in your mind, I know you'll agree to the marriage."

Chitrangada looked into her father's eyes which were the exact shade of coal black as her own. "What if I get a younger groom? Someone who is rich too. Will you agree to that match?" She challenged her father.

"Do you really have someone in your mind? Or are you just talking in the air?" Bikram asked her in a casual voice even though he was quaking within. Harischandra Gajanan would make a terrible enemy and Bikram had already taken one crore rupees from him, most of which he had spent by now. They both had even signed an agreement that Bikram would give his daughter's hand in marriage to Harischandra while the latter would pay a total of four more crores, half on the day of the engagement and the other half after the wedding ceremony.

While Harischandra knew for a fact that the agreement would not really hold good in any court of law since Chitrangada was an adult, he had not cared to enlighten Bikram who did not know the nuances. Bikram thought that his daughter was his property and it was her duty to listen to whatever he told her.

For a minute, Chitrangada was tempted to tell her father about Raj. But then, what could she tell him about her roommate of three days? How chivalrous he had been? How he had never thought of taking advantage of her despite the two of them being cooped up in one suite with no way to escape from each other's company? How it was only later, because of her proximity in his bed, that he had made love to her, that too since she had as good as invited him to? How he had been so helpful even if he had teased her mercilessly? How handsome he was? But then, while she knew that he was based in Udaipur, she did not even know his surname. Nor if Raj was his real name.

She shook her head slowly now, a sad expression on her face. "No Dad. I don't have anyone in mind. But I'm sure I'll find someone before long." She lifted her gaze to his defiantly.

"Don't be an idiot, Chitra. You can't find a better man than Harischandra; take your old dad's word for it. He will make you a wonderful husband. You…" He went on and on, extolling the non-existent virtues of the man he had chosen for his son-in-law, not really bothered that he had lost his daughter's attention completely.

Raj had mentioned that he was taking part in the Snow Polo World Cup at St Moritz. Chitrangada sat up straight. That match must have got over last weekend. Surely, she will be able to find out more on the internet. But… but what was the use? She could find out more about him, but that did not mean she planned to contact Raj. The situation today was no different from that morning when she left his hotel suite without leaving her name or number for him to find her. And that had been because he had left her with no hope of a future with him.

But once the idea had taken root in her mind, Chitrangada could not let it go. She wanted to find out all about the man she had fallen in love with. "Dad," she got up from the dining table, "I just remembered that I have some urgent work to finish. I'll catch you at lunch." She walked in a rush towards the central staircase and raced up the steps to go to her room. She needed to get to her laptop urgently. Yes, it did not matter if she only got to stalk Raj on the internet. Chitrangada felt a powerful urge to get closer to him, even if it was only via the World Wide Web.

Bikram got up to walk towards the library, shaking his head to himself. Well, he supposed he should not complain. While she had protested, Chitrangada had not exactly refused to marry Harischandra.

Chitrangada was in a frenzy as she waited for her laptop to boot. She quickly opened a screen to search for last week's snow polo match. Her jaw dropped when she saw the main picture that was thrown up. It was Raj holding the winning cup aloft, flanked by his team members, a wide grin on his face. Her eyes sought the deep grooves on his cheeks as she traced their shape on the screen with a trembling finger. He looked so endearingly familiar. How she had missed him during the rest of her stay in Zurich!

She lowered her eyes to the caption which read: Rajvardhan Thakore and his men win the World Cup. So, that was his full name!

She read the article till the end, her heart beating a wild tattoo, before searching for him by name. Besides his social media accounts, she found many articles featuring him and his elder brother Indrajeet Thakore. Raj or Rajvardhan was from the royal household of the Thakores from Rajasthan. He was the second son of the family. Educated at Harvard, he had been playing polo since the past seven years. He had been living and working in the USA and was planning to shift back to India by the end of the month. Raj had celebrated his twenty-eighth birthday four months ago.

Chitrangada searched a lot more, checking out the many news snippets to find out if he had a girlfriend. He had told her that he had no one, but there was some woman or the other hanging on to his arm at every social event he had been photographed at.

As she scrolled through more images, she stopped suddenly, seeing a familiar face. Or rather, a face that seemed as if she had known it forever. Could it be her childhood friend Yashodhara? She clicked on the picture to read the caption, after checking out the picture of the man standing next to her, his arm around her waist. It was Indrajeet Thakore, the eldest son of the Thakore royals.

And, she had been right about the lady in the picture. It was her long-lost friend Yashodhara. Her heart beating wildly with excitement, Chitrangada read the article until the end. Doing a few more searches, she found out that her dearest friend had moved to England after leaving school and had only recently returned a few years ago. And she was married to Raj's elder brother of all the people in the world.

Coming to a sudden decision, Chitrangada got up from her chair after shutting her laptop. It was time to reunite with her best friend.

7

Indrajeet Thakore walked into his home after stabling his horse, just in time for breakfast. But before that, he had to check on his wife Yashodhara. He had left her in bed when he had gone for a solo ride at 5.30 in the morning. She was in the first trimester of her pregnancy and had been having fainting spells in the mornings over the last few days.

"Jeet." He turned when he heard his wife calling out to him from the direction of the dining room just as he placed his foot on the first step. Making an about turn, he spoke even as he walked towards her, "What are you doing downstairs, Yash? You were supposed to be resting." He caught her in his arms and held her close to his chest even as he bent his head to kiss her deeply.

Yashodhara pressed her cheek close to his heart, a smile on her face. "My darling husband, let me explain something to you. I'm pregnant with your child, not suffering from some terminal illness." There was amusement in her voice as she lifted her head to look into his eyes, her expression adoring. She loved him more than any other human being in the world. She wondered if she would be able to give half as much love to their child growing in her womb. But then, it was Indrajeet who had saved her from herself and had made her whole.

"Very funny," said her husband now, studying her pale face. "Does that mean you're feeling better?"

"Of course. The sickness lasts only for a short while on waking up. Otherwise, I'm right as rain."

He studied her face for a few more moments until he heard the firm tread of footsteps, reluctantly letting go of her, giving her a mock frown when she laughed softly.

"Good morning, Pappa," he called out to his father, Raja Gajendar Thakore.

"Good morning, Jeet, Yasho. So, what's for breakfast today?" Gajendar walked into the dining room to sit down at the head of the table.

"*Pyaaz ki kachori* and *dal pakwaan*," said Rani Ragini Devi, wiping her hands on a towel as she stepped out of the kitchen.

"I thought we were on a diet." Gajendar teased his wife. "Are you sure we can eat all those fried stuff?"

Ragini looked at her husband's mischievous face with a smile on her own. "First thing in the morning, yes. The meals get lighter as the day wears on." She turned to her eldest born and asked, "Jeet, did you speak to Raj? When is he coming home?"

"The day after tomorrow, Mamma."

"I'm so glad that he's returning for good this time round," said Ragini, who liked to have all her children about her. It would be another year before Dayanita, her youngest born, would return home from her studies in the USA.

They sat down to breakfast and chatted their way through it until a bell rang loudly. Yashodhara got up immediately. "That must be Grandma wanting her tea."

"Why don't you sit down? I'll take it to her," offered Indrajeet, already on his feet.

Yashodhara frowned at her husband. "You know that she doesn't like it when you take her tea as you insist on carrying the tray yourself. You need to remember that you are a Prince." There was laughter in her voice as she told her husband that.

Gajendar laughed. "Why don't you both do something, Yasho? You walk ahead and let Jeet carry the tea tray. Only give me a few moments to hide behind a pillar in mother's room. I don't want to miss the fun."

"You're on, Pappa," said Indrajeet, taking the tray that Ramlal was holding patiently in his hands.

"I don't know what you men see in rattling Mother first thing in the morning," muttered Ragini. Her mother-in-law, Rajmata Santhini Devi, liked to behave as if she was still the reigning queen of the Thakore Royal household, not to miss the affinity she held towards the British. It never seemed to matter to her that India had attained independence before she was born and had become a republic when she was but a toddler.

"Good morning, Grandma," greeted Yashodhara, walking into Santhini Devi's chamber.

"Good morning, child. Tell me, how have you been this morning?" The old matriarch's voice was gruff as she greeted her favourite granddaughter-in-law. She liked Yashodhara for two reasons. One was because it was the Rajmata who had chosen her for her eldest grandson's bride. Another was because Indrajeet was also her favourite grandchild.

"I'm doing absolutely fine, Grandma." Yashodhara pulled the curtains to the side, letting sunlight into the dark bedroom.

"Good morning, Grandma dear," called out Indrajeet, placing the tea tray on a small table before lifting it on to the bed in front of Santhini Devi as she reclined against her bedhead.

"Indrajeet, why are you playing footman today? Has Ramlal taken ill or something?" There was a deep scowl on Santhini Devi's face as she glared at her grandson.

"Tch, Grandma, what kind of a greeting is that?" Indrajeet stepped forward to give his grandmother a hug before planting a kiss on her wrinkled forehead. "Don't I get a polite 'good morning' like the one Yash received? Some people are so lucky."

"Indrajeet!" Santhini Devi punched her grandson's muscular arm with a wrinkled fist. "I asked you a question."

"What was that now?" He sat next to her on the bed, patting the space next to him invitingly to his wife.

"Is Ramlal taken ill?"

"From when have you been bothered about the staff's welfare?" asked Indrajeet, giving his grandmother a mocking look.

"Yashodhara, tell your husband from me to get out of my sight, right this minute," said the old matriarch, her voice dripping with ice. "I'll not tolerate disrespect nor will I put up with his plebeian airs. I'll talk to him only when he behaves like a prince should."

Yashodhara bit her lip to stop herself from laughing outright, surreptitiously eyeing her father-in-law who was standing just outside the door, quaking with laughter as he followed the conversation. "Jeet, will you please leave? You're bothering Grandma."

"Exactly." Santhini Devi refused to look at Indrajeet as she lifted her cup of tea and began to sip from it, her small finger lifted in the air.

"Please accept my sincere apologies, Grandma." Indrajeet took her left hand in his to raise it to his lips as he pressed a kiss to the back of it. "You know how much I love you, don't you, Grandma?"

"Yes, I know all that. Get off, now. And next time, let the servants do their work. You have your duties as the prince." She gave her grandson a mock glare. "So, when is Rajvardhan returning home?"

"The day after tomorrow. Do you miss him badly?" Indrajeet grinned at Santhini Devi.

"Bah! That brat! Never. To be truthful, this house is going to be in a state of war when he comes to live here permanently. Can't stand the boy," declared Santhini Devi vehemently.

"How can you say that, Grandma? Raj is your grandson too," Yashodhara could not help protesting. During the two years since her marriage to Indrajeet, she had met her brother-in-law a few times, that too only briefly. But she knew that he was a charming young man, as hard-working as his brother and well-mannered too. She did not really understand why Grandma didn't like Rajvardhan.

"That he is. But he's also the devil incarnate." Santhini Devi appeared wicked when she declared that, much to Gajendar's amusement. He knew for a fact that while his eldest son, Indrajeet, took after his father, Raja Devendar Thakore, who was no more; his younger son, Rajvardhan, was exactly like his mother, Rajmata Santhini Devi Thakore. It was no wonder that they were at constant loggerheads. They were both too much like each other.

A servant knocked on the door just then before announcing that there was a visitor asking for Princess Yashodhara.

"Excuse me, Grandma," said Yashodhara, getting up from the bed immediately. "Will you be needing anything else?"

"Nothing for now, child. You go on and allow me to drink my tea in peace." Santhini Devi dismissed them all with a flick of her hand.

Chitrangada stood in the middle of the hall of the Thakore palace, her heart in her throat. Will her childhood friend remember her? After all, it had been fourteen years since they had set eyes on one another.

"Chitra!" Yashodhara yelled, breaking into a run as she crossed the length of the hall before throwing her arms around Chitrangada, her eyes damp with tears. "It has been so long."

The friends hugged each other before Yashodhara dragged Chitrangada on to a sofa, her arm still around her. Remembering her manners, she introduced her childhood friend to her parents-in-law and her husband.

The sensitive Indrajeet immediately realised that the two women needed privacy. After all, they had to catch up on the past fourteen years of their lives.

"Lovely meeting you, Princess Chitrangada Vasudeva. I hope you'll join us for lunch. Yash, do you want to sit in the library with your friend? I'm sure you both need to catch up on a lot of stuff. I'll take myself off to check on Raj's horse farm and return in time for lunch."

Yashodhara nodded, a smile on her face. Chitrangada did not miss the love shining out of her friend's eyes for her husband. She had also not missed the fact that Indrajeet was going to check on Raj's horse farm. His words somehow made Raj seem more real, someone who actually lived in this palace, right here in Udaipur. Her heart beat all the faster for hearing his name on his brother's lips.

The friends chatted and chatted some more, sipping coffee and munching on home-made cookies that Ramlal brought in. They had to catch up on fourteen years' worth of what had happened in both their lives. Chitrangada teared up when she heard all about the trauma that Yashodhara had undergone at the young age of twelve; how she had lived with it in silence until Indrajeet had brought everything out into the open after they were married and finally the healing had happened.

"I so wanted to be in touch with you, Chitra. But mamma—please don't hate her for it—didn't want me to talk to anyone I knew down here. That's why she insisted that I studied in England. Please forgive me for disappearing from your life."

Chitrangada pressed her hand over Yashodhara's mouth, stopping her from talking. "Don't. You shouldn't apologise for what is no fault of yours. All I can say is that I missed you terribly."

"So, what's happening in your life? Are you planning to get married? Or rather, is Bikram uncle arranging your wedding with someone?" Yashodhara wanted to know all about her friend's personal life once she got to know about her professional one.

Chitrangada's lips drooped; her expression bitter. "That's a long story. Let me bring you up to date."

Yashodhara listened to all about Chitrangada's imminent betrothal to Raja Harischandra Gajanan with shock on her face. "But why would your father do that? There are so many eligible bachelors, much younger men who would be better suited to marry you. Let me talk to Indrajeet. And by the way, my brother-in-law, Rajvardhan, is twenty-eight. He's tall, dark and handsome. You met my husband. Raj resembles him a lot."

Chitrangada had the most difficult time holding the rising colour back from her face. Just hearing his name was making her heartbeat go wild. Will she get to meet him anytime soon? Then again, what will the meeting with Raj achieve? What if his interest in her had been passing? Her mind went back and forth as she oscillated between hope and despair.

Just now, she gave her friend a vague nod, not saying anything in response as she felt too choked.

But Yashodhara was excited at the prospect of arranging a match between her brother-in-law and her best friend. Wouldn't it just be wonderful if Chitrangada came to live at Jadeja palace as the second daughter-in-law of the house?!

"Can't you stop your father from going ahead with this alliance with Raja Gajanan?" Yashodhara asked. "I'm sure Bikram uncle will see logic once you convince him. The man is definitely too old for you."

Chitrangada groaned. "I have told him once if I have told him a hundred times that it's a match made in hell." She sat up, her back straight, a determined thrust to her chin. "Of course, I haven't given up yet." Now that she knew from Yashodhara that Raj—Rajvardhan—was returning home soon, should she try to get in touch with him? She would need to think it through. She had her pride. What if she found out that he did not give a damn about what was happening in her life? Will she be able to take the outright rejection? Damn, and a double damn!

Yashodhara changed the subject to pleasanter things, a smile in her eyes. She liked her own idea of a match between Rajvardhan and Chitrangada. She planned to set things in motion soon by talking to her husband later that night. Let her brother-in-law get back home and settle in first. She was determined to do her best to kill two birds with one stone—get Harischandra Gajanan out of the picture and reinstate Rajvardhan in his place as her best friend's life partner.

What neither woman realised was that Bikram Vasudeva was equally, if not more determined, that the marriage between his daughter and Raja Harischandra Gajanan should take place. He was ready to stoop to any level for the same, as Chitrangada found out to her shock the very next week.

8

ajvardhan tried to sleep on the flight back home. It should not have been so difficult as he was travelling business class. But one face kept coming up in front of his mind's eye, making it difficult for him to relax.

Princess!

Why the hell had he not asked her for her phone number? Had it been pride? Ego? Or had it been the fact that she had spoken to him about her upcoming engagement? What had stopped him from taking her contact details?

But that had been before they made love. She had been such a responsive lover, matching his passion totally. He could not help smiling when he recalled her enthusiasm. It was the second time they made love. She had wanted to know all about his body which was so different from hers.

Rajvardhan's smile disappeared as he sighed. Why had she upped and left that morning, without even waiting to tell him bye?

He had browsed on the internet, searching for Princess. It was like looking for a needle in a haystack. He was not even sure if that was her name. Why had he not even clicked a selfie with her? They had been too busy with other things—like exploring one another's body—to bother with taking pictures.

Then there was her impending engagement. While Princess had not seemed too happy when she mentioned it, she had been clear that it was going to happen. If that were the case, maybe it was guilt. She must have felt guilty and had decided to run away, rather than face her lover of two nights. If that were the case, he had better stop thinking—no, mooning— about her the way he had been doing since the day she disappeared from his life.

Rajvardhan had reached that logical conclusion only early that morning, just before sleep finally claimed him.

Then why the hell was he thinking of her now? Shouldn't he just forget all about her and get on with his life?

Tell that to his heart! It just refused to listen. It was only after Princess had walked out of his hotel suite that he had realised that she had taken a part of him— his heart—along with her. By then it had been too late.

Rajvardhan moved restlessly, before switching on the screen in front of him. He might as well watch a film as sleep was nowhere near coming. Wearing the headphones, he sat back to catch *Jerry Maguire* starring Tom Cruise. He did not know when he actually dropped off to sleep, opening his eyes only when he felt a hand on his shoulder, shaking him awake.

"We should be landing at the Delhi airport soon, sir," said the air-hostess respectfully, her eyes brightening as she took in his tousled hair and handsome face.

"Thanks," he said, his eyes crinkling as he gave her a charming smile. "Are you still serving coffee?"

"Of course, sir. Let me get you a cup."

He got up to go to the bathroom to refresh himself before returning to his seat to have the black coffee that the air-hostess had brought him.

He was one of the first people to get off the flight. He had a connecting flight to Udaipur in an hour and a half.

It was nine in the morning when the car that had picked Rajvardhan at the Udaipur airport entered the Thakore palace grounds. Ragini Devi came hurrying to the entrance to hug her second child. "I'm so happy to have you home, Raj," she said, her voice wobbling with emotion.

Rajvardhan hugged his diminutive mother, pressing his lips to the top of her head. "I'm glad to be back home too, Mamma. How have you been? And where's Pappa?" he asked, his eyes searching for his father and the rest of the family.

"Welcome home, Raj," said Gajendar, walking into the palace from a side entrance, obviously having been puttering in the garden, his most favourite pastime.

"Pappa." Rajvardhan hugged his father in turn.

"Really proud of you my son, for winning the snow polo event at St Moritz."

Rajvardhan grinned, bumping a fist with Indrajeet as his elder brother walked up to him. "Thanks, Pappa. It was good fun." His face darkened when he recalled the time he had spent with Princess. He could not help but mentally curse himself for not having a way to get in touch with her. "And congratulations, Jeet. I'm so excited about becoming an uncle soon. When's the baby due?"

Indrajeet laughed, hugging his younger brother. "It's still a long way to go. Yash is due to deliver by end of September."

Rajvardhan nodded, turning to greet his sister-in-law, giving her a hug too as he congratulated her. He felt a trace of envy towards his brother as he watched the two of them holding hands. Giving himself a mental shake, he walked along with everyone to the dining room for breakfast.

"So, how's the old tyrant?" he asked, munching his way into his favourite *aloo paratha*.

Ragini shushed him. "What a way to talk about your grandmother, Raj? Do have some respect."

Indrajeet laughed along with his brother before answering his question, "Grandma is doing very well, bossing over everyone. Her usual self."

Gajendar listened to his sons' chatter, not saying much, his eyes darting from one to the other as he kept track of what they were talking about.

Rajvardhan turned to his mother and said, "Mamma, you're too nice. But Grandma is something else altogether. She…"

"That's all very well, Raj. But that still doesn't mean that you speak disrespectfully about your grandmother." Ragini scolded her younger son, a smile on her face. "After all, she's given birth to your Pappa."

"I did wonder why you tolerated her all these years. And now I know," teased Rajvardhan, "she gave birth to the love of your life."

A blushing Ragini threw her cloth napkin at her grown up son, unable to control her laughter. How she had missed him and his mischievous ways!

Gajendar joined in the laughter, even as he gazed at his wife in adoration.

Rajvardhan got up from the dining table. "Let me go meet the old lady and tell her that I've arrived. I'm sure she must be so looking forward to my return home," he said, winking at Indrajeet and Yashodhara.

Yashodhara laughed on hearing that, recalling Santhini Devi's words the day before yesterday. "Of course, Raj. She has been waiting eagerly to cross swords with you. Grandma has been missing that a lot."

"You said it, Yasho," said Rajvardhan, pointing his index finger in her direction even as he tilted his head in agreement.

Walking up the staircase, he went into his room and rummaged in his luggage to take a bottle of premium Scotch whiskey that he had bought especially for his grandmother at the duty-free shop and a newly launched perfume that he had purchased in the USA. Armed with the two items, he walked into Santhini Devi's chamber, calling out, "Good morning, my darling Grandma, I'm home, and for good this time."

He walked up to where she was sitting on the bed sipping her tea. Placing her gifts on the bed near her feet, he hugged her, before pressing his lips to her forehead. "How have you been?"

"Not too bad until now," she grumbled, giving her younger grandson a mock glare. She would never admit even at gun point that she believed that Rajvardhan was the handsomest of her grandchildren.

"And why is that?" he asked her, lying down on the bed, next to her.

"Rajvardhan Thakore, you very well know that I don't like it if you lie down on my bed, especially with your shoes on." Santhini Devi scolded him.

"Okay, *baba*, whatever you say," said Rajvardhan, getting up to tug his shoes off before lying down once again.

She sighed dramatically. "Rajvardhan…"

"Before you get on your high horse, Grandma, do you want to see what I've got for you?"

"Rajvardhan Thakore, listen to me. First of all, I don't like being interrupted. And secondly…"

"…you don't like me to lie on your bed, especially with my shoes on. Grandma, stop being a pain and lighten up. I didn't mean to interrupt, but you know only too well that I don't like being lectured and I was forced to cut you short only because of that. As for lying on your bed, see for yourself. You are still in bed. I'm just lying on the other half. How does that bother you?"

Santhini Devi fumed, her brown eyes sparking furiously at him. So typical! "Rajvardhan, you don't listen to anyone and have no respect for your elders. Your parents have spoilt you rotten." She paused to catch her breath.

Rajvardhan jumped up to sit next to her before whispering in her ear, "Grandma, are you by any chance describing yourself?"

"Huh?!" Santhini Devi gave him a shrewd look before her lips parted in a rare smile. Soon, she was laughing. Drat the boy! He could not have been more right.

"Grandma, you're truly grand," said Rajvardhan, hugging her once again. He lifted the parcels and handed them to her one by one. "I hope you like them."

"Blue label? That's my boy. I love it," she declared before reaching out for the second parcel. Running her hands over the rectangular parcel and shaking it gently, she said, "It's a perfume."

"So why don't you open it and find out if you like it?" Rajvardhan stretched on the bed beside her, his hands stacked under his head as he eyed her lazily.

Santhini Devi meticulously peeled off the gift wrap and opened the box that contained the bottle of Ralph Lauren Polo perfume and sprayed a drop on her wrist. Raising her hand to her nose, she took a sniff and said, "This is really good, Rajvardhan. I only wish you had bought a bigger bottle." Typically, she did not have it in her heart to pay a fulsome compliment.

Not that Rajvardhan was bothered by it. He knew his grandmother only too well and loved her despite her nature. "No worries, Grandma. I'll get you all you want. Just give me a week's warning, is all I ask."

"Take yourself off now. I need to get up and get ready for the day."

"What's the rush?" asked Rajvardhan, his eyes half-closed as he stretched lazily. "I'm sleepy, Grandma. Do you have an appointment or what?"

"Rajvardhan Thakore! Will you take yourself off to your own room, right now?"

"Okay, okay, you old tyrant!" Rajvardhan got up. "There's no need to shout or throw your weight around. I'm going."

"Wash your mouth with some phenol on your way." Santhini Devi called out as he walked out of her chamber, determined to have the last word, shaking her head when she heard him laugh, a smile on her face.

Yashodhara caught Rajvardhan on the corridor outside his room. "I want a word with you, Raj."

"Sure, Yasho. Come on in." He invited her into his room. He dug some more into his suitcase and brought out a few packets. "I know it's too early, but I couldn't help shopping for some baby stuff. Here you go." He placed the parcels on a table in front of her.

Yashodhara laughed softly, colour on her cheeks. "You're worse than Jeet. He's already checked out a few ponies for the baby."

Rajvardhan paused in his search for some more gifts that he had packed in his luggage, to look at his sister-in-law. "No way is he going to get a pony for my nephew or niece from somewhere else. What's the use of running a horse farm if I can't provide a pony for the baby?"

"Good question," said Yashodhara, her eyes crinkling as she grinned at her brother-in-law. "Why don't you ask your brother that?"

"I will. And tell me, how's your health? All going good?"

"Perfectly, Raj, thank you. Er... I wanted to ask you something."

"Oh yeah. Shoot!" Rajvardhan sat next to her on the sofa, all attention as he waited for her to talk.

"I have a close friend; her name is Chitrangada. She's the Vasudeva princess from Jodhana, the only child of Raja Bikram Vasudeva."

Raj nodded, clenching his jaw when he heard his sister-in-law utter the word 'princess'. What was Yashodhara getting at?

Yashodhara plodded on, determined to have her say, despite not seeing any kind of enthusiasm on her brother-in-law's face. "She's twenty-five and simply beautiful. She's also well-educated and a career woman. I was thinking…" she paused, wondering if maybe she should ask Indrajeet to do the talking.

"What were you thinking?" Rajvardhan was scowling now. If he had understood correctly, Yashodhara was doing a spot of matchmaking on his behalf. *Why the hell can't people mind their own business?* he thought, in a fit of temper that flared up from nowhere.

Looking at the stony expression on his face, Yashodhara decided to make a hasty retreat. "Nothing that can't wait, Raj. I suppose you must be tired. We can talk about it later." She got up to leave.

No! He couldn't just let her walk out like that. Yashodhara was sweet and always friendly. Moreover, she was pregnant. Rajvardhan knew that he must have hurt her by his behaviour. "I'm sorry, Yasho. Didn't mean to be rude. But just now, I am in no state to think of marriage. And that's what you were going to say, right? A match between your friend and me."

Yashodhara brightened when he apologised only to feel bad when she heard him out fully. She shrugged. She had tried, hadn't she? "I hope everything is alright with you, Raj."

She was startled when she heard the long sigh from him. Tucking his hands into the pockets of his jeans, Rajvardhan turned away to walk towards the window that overlooked the lawn. "Nothing that can't be set right soon, Yasho. No worries."

How he wished that he could believe his own words!

9

Two days after her meeting with Yashodhara, Chitrangada was in her room, setting up her schedule for the whole month. Sitting at the window, she took her eyes off the laptop to stare outside, sipping from a cup of coffee. The view from her room never ceased to lift her mood. It faced the garden behind the Vasudeva palace that abounded with trees and shrubs, with a fish pond in the middle. Lilies of many colours floated on the pond, adding colour to the scene.

Her mind automatically went to Raj. His full name might be Rajvardhan, but he would always be Raj to her. The time she had spent with him in Zurich had simply been out of this world, the very air around them sizzling with chemistry. Her body broke out in goose bumps whenever she thought of their time together.

If she got to tie the knot with him, it would truly be a dream come true. While the chances appeared too slim as of now, it did not stop Chitrangada from dreaming of it. But even if she never set eyes on Raj again, she still did not want to marry the man her father had chosen for her. Just now, the thought of marriage with anyone seemed anathema to her.

Somehow, she had to convince her father to call off her engagement and subsequent marriage to Raja Harischandra Gajanan. It was going to be a task and a difficult one at that. But Chitrangada was determined. She would somehow make her father see her point of view.

Just then, there was a knock on her door. Her maid, Kavita, walked in to say that Raja Harischandra Gajanan had arrived and that her father wanted her to go downstairs immediately.

Chitrangada scowled, saying, "Oh shit! Tell Dad that I should be down in twenty minutes." What the hell was the old man doing here at her home? There was still three weeks to go before their supposed engagement. He gave her the creeps. But knowing her father, she knew that she could not escape the meeting. Why the hell did she have to be working from home today of all days? But then, she had set aside today for planning the next few weeks.

Chitrangada looked in the mirror. She was casually dressed in jeans and a t-shirt, both faithfully following the shape of her lissom figure. She swiftly got out of her clothes and draped herself in a sari and a blouse that covered her from neck to waist, ensuring that not an inch of her midriff showed. She piled her hair into a knot on the top of her head that added inches to her tall frame before applying light make up. She took out some heavy jewellery and wore the necklace, earrings, and bracelet before slipping her dainty feet into four-inch heels.

Talk about power dressing!

Her plan was to tower over the old goat who planned to marry her. Her height of five feet, ten inches, plus her top knot, along with the high-heeled shoes; made her a few inches taller than Raja Harischandra Gajanan. She hoped that it would dent his massive ego, enough for him to stay away from her—forever, hopefully.

Chitrangada made her way down the marble staircase and walked over to knock on the door to the library. She entered when she heard her father's voice, telling her to, "Come in."

"Come in, Chitra. See who has made the time to come and meet you amidst his busy schedule!" Bikram Vasudeva gushed as he took his daughter's hand to guide her towards their esteemed guest, his gaze approving as he noticed the effort Chitrangada had put in to make herself presentable.

Harischandra got up from the deep armchair he had been sitting in, his steely grey gaze roving over the beautiful princess who was soon to be his wife. His slightly protruding eyes gleamed with excitement as he was instantly aroused by her beauty and proximity. Three weeks to the engagement and some more months to the wedding. Why the hell had he agreed to Bikram's dictates? "Hello, my dear. How have you been?"

Chitrangada walked forward before stopping two feet short of where he was standing, hoping to keep as far away from him as was decently possible, considering that they were going to be betrothed soon. She put out a hand to him, pleased to note that her eyes were on a level with the top of his head.

What she did not expect was for Harischandra to move forward to give her a squeeze, making sure she felt his hard on, giving her a strong urge to puke. She squirmed, trying to wiggle out of his arms which were surprisingly strong. When she realised that her movements only seemed to excite him more, making him grow bigger against her body, she stopped struggling.

"That's better, my sweet," whispered Harischandra into her ear, "it's time you learned to abide by my wishes, unless you want to be badly hurt."

Was he threatening her? Chitrangada saw red. Biting her lower lip to curb her temper, she waited for him to release her, her hands clenched into tight fists. It was due to her father's presence that she refrained from thrusting her knee where it really would have hurt him. She would have even succeeded in bringing down his ardour. The thought made her want to giggle wildly, making her almost choke as she tried to control the urge.

Harischandra placed both his hands on her slim shoulders to move her a few inches away from him when he thought he heard her make a strangled noise. But her face was blank when he stared at it, her lids half closed over her beautiful eyes. He ran his eyes avidly over the top of her body, pleased to notice her luscious breasts rise and fall as she took deep breaths. So! She was not exactly immune to him. Her reaction also suggested a depth of passion. He grinned, pleased with himself as he rubbed his lower body once more against her soft frame before letting her go.

It promised to be fun, breaking this filly!

Totally revolted, Chitrangada moved back to almost fall into a sofa. She managed to sit back, crossing her legs. She could not wait to run back to her room and have a cleansing bath after being pawed by this… this animal. She refused to contribute to the conversation between her father and Harischandra, even when she had to endure a long five-course lunch with the lecher. It was a good thing that she was not left alone with him.

Finally, Harischandra got up to take his leave at four in the evening. Chitrangada stepped away nimbly when he would have hugged her again, not missing the fury which burst into his steely grey eyes. She just did not care.

"That went off so well," said Bikram, rubbing his hands together in pleasure, completely unaware of his daughter's temper that was waiting to blow out of control. "The Raja so obviously adores you. I really didn't expect him to make a visit today. But I suppose he has been missing you." He laughed as he said that, looking at his Chitrangada proudly, before turning to check out the large bag their guest had brought over as gift.

"Dad!" Her voice came out louder than she had meant it to, but Chitrangada was beyond caring. This farce had gone too far. She had hoped to talk to her father at the right time, when he was in a more relaxed mood, to call a halt to the impending engagement. But Harischandra's visit had brought things to a head. Once she had her father's complete attention on her, she continued, "Leave that bag alone. I want that sent right back to Raja Gajanan."

Bikram frowned at her. "What's wrong with you, Chitra? The Raja has brought it for you, with so much love. How can you throw it back on his face?"

"Do you hear yourself, Dad? And did you really see the two of us together? Do you really think we would make a lovely married couple? He's old, Dad, and a lecher at that. He pawed me, literally. I…"

"Shut up, Chitra. I'll not hear one more word from you, not if you mean to insult your *fiancé*. You have become too spoilt, it seems. Enough now. Don't you dare speak another word against the kind and generous Raja. I wouldn't stand for it."

Chitrangada stared at her father, wondering if he had become completely senile. "But, Dad…" she raised her hands up in front of her placatingly when she saw the deepening of his frown, "okay, okay, I won't say anything to insult the man. But, listen Dad, I don't want to marry him. I…" she stopped, concluding that it was not the right time to talk about Raj, especially since she did not know if the Thakore scion was interested in her at all, "I need more time, Dad. I don't want to marry so soon."

Bikram sighed, calming down a bit. He walked up to his daughter and threw an arm around her shoulders. "That's not a problem, child. We are only going to have the engagement now. The wedding can be performed in September. That gives you more than six months."

Chitrangada's lips drooped. She shuddered when she recalled Harischandra's body thrust against hers. If he had his way, he would simply rape her even before they got married. She was sure of it. And it was obvious that her father planned to hand over the license to him with *band baajaa*. It was time for some straight talking.

"Listen, Dad. I've never crossed you all these years and have always given in to your wishes. I…"

"That's only because I've always been extra sensitive to your wishes and needs and have never stopped you from doing what you wanted." Her father interrupted her.

Chitrangada nodded her dark head. What he said was true. But right now, this was a life changing situation for her. He was trying to marry her off to someone who made her skin crawl in revulsion. "I agree, Dad. And that's exactly the reason I'm appealing to you. Please reconsider. I understand that you think that the Raja is a grand match for me. But believe me,

Dad, there are many others who may be better suited. If it's difficult for you to find a groom for me, allow me to do the honours. A little bit of time is what I ask." Chitrangada was pleading by now, not missing the stony expression on her father's face.

"I have given you enough time, till end of this month before your engagement and six more months before your wedding. But otherwise, I refuse to listen to you. Raja Harischandra is the perfect groom for you and I don't plan to change my mind." He walked away from her to sit behind his work desk, leaning on his leather swivel chair with a finality.

Chitrangada rose to her full height, her small chin thrust out in determination. "Well, let me also tell you what my decision is. And before that, let me remind you that I'm twenty-five years old and an adult. You can't force me to marry a man that I don't like. Yeah, I know this is your house, while I'm also aware that this palace belonged to a long line of Vasudeva royals, my ancestors. But I don't plan to be a pain in your neck. I'll take myself out of your hair and go live my life, the way I want. If you ever find it in your heart to forgive me, we can continue as father and daughter, as always. Goodbye!"

Just as she turned to leave, she heard her father say, "Just a minute, before you go." She turned around and blanched, the colour completely draining out of her face as she stared at the pistol that her father held in his hand. "Don't worry, I won't kill you as I'm not such a cruel father. But," he turned to place the barrel of the pistol against his right temple, his eyes steady, "that doesn't mean that I can't kill myself." He could not tell his daughter how desperate he was. He might as well die rather than cancel this alliance. If he had not paid them from the money he had received from Raja Gajanan, the loan sharks would have done away with him. Now that he had spent the money, if the wedding did not happen, Harischandra would definitely kill him. Whichever way, it seemed that Bikram was not going to live very long. *Might as well kill myself,* he thought dramatically. Or, just maybe, his daughter would agree to the wedding if she realised that he was even prepared to die for it.

"Daddyyyyyyy," Chitrangada screamed, rushing towards her father, her heels making no noise as she ran headlong across the carpet. She grabbed his hand, pulling the pistol and throwing it far away from them. She hugged him, tears pouring down her eyes. "Don't, Dad. I'll do whatever you want."

She didn't notice the triumphant smile on Bikram's face as she buried her face in his shoulder and cried, like a small child, her temper and stubbornness disappearing like mist in front of her father's diabolic act.

Yashodhara cuddled against her husband's warmth, completely satiated by their lovemaking. The days when she used to be scared of a physical relationship were long past, all thanks to Indrajeet. He had been patience personified as he wooed his wife during the first few months of their marriage.

"Jeet."

"Hmm…" Indrajeet was half asleep, his head buried against his wife's breasts. He was too comfortable to want to move.

"I was thinking… are you listening?"

He smiled against her body, refusing to move. "Hmm."

"Very funny." Yashodhara tilted her head to take a nip of his golden shoulder, making Indrajeet laugh lazily.

"Now that has woken up not just my brain, but also other parts of me." He moved back to lie on the bed, pulling her over his chest. "Tell me."

"I was just wondering; what do you think of a match between Raj and my friend Chitrangada?"

He looked at her lovely face, enquiry on his. "But I thought your friend is going to be engaged soon. Or is that wrong?"

Yashodhara sighed, an unhappy expression on her face. "That's right. But still…"

"Yash, you got to meet Princess Chitrangada after such a long time. Are you sure you know her as she is today? Is it okay to interfere with such an important decision of her life?"

Her lips drooped. "I know Chitra and she hasn't changed at all. Okay, she's grown up now. But I'm sure you know what I mean. And Jeet, she isn't happy with this alliance. She's marrying a man who's her father's peer. I…"

"What?" Indrajeet was startled enough to get up and sit against the headboard. "Really! But why would she agree to such a marriage?"

"That's exactly what I've been thinking too." Yashodhara rose up to snuggle on his chest, rubbing her silky cheek against it, revelling in the rough texture. "She did mention that she's going to do her best to dissuade her father. But when I spoke to her today afternoon, she told me that she's going ahead with the match as she didn't want to go against her father's wishes."

"If that's the case, then there's nothing we can do about it, is there?" He kissed the top of her head, his arms going around her as he held her close.

Yashodhara sighed again. "That's what I keep telling myself. But, Jeet, Chitra is upset. I know that for a fact."

He tilted her chin to look into her eyes. "What do you want to do? How do you think you can get Raj interested in your friend or your friend interested in him?"

Yashodhara got up to sit straight, delicate colour blooming on her cheeks when she caught her husband's avid gaze on her body. "Well, we've been invited for the engagement on the thirtieth. I was thinking if you could persuade Raj to join us…"

Indrajeet grinned, reaching a hand to tweak the tip of a breast. "You have it all planned out. It's just that I can see only one hurdle here. Raj won't agree to go with us. Mamma has the devil's own time getting him to go to weddings and other ceremonies at relatives' homes. If it's his friends then he's always ready. But then, that's how he is." He grimaced.

"Even if you ask him to?"

"Why don't you talk to Raj about Chitra? See if he shows any kind of interest at all," Indrajeet told Yashodhara. "It just might work."

She was shaking her head even before he finished the sentence, recalling the conversation she had had with her brother-in-law regarding his marriage. "I have. He didn't sound enthusiastic about it, not at all."

"There you go then. If Raj isn't interested, he just isn't. There isn't much one can do about it." As far as he was concerned, that ended the matter. Indrajeet moved closer to her to capture a swollen nipple in his mouth, rubbing his tongue across it repeatedly until Yashodhara forgot her own name.

He made love to her lazily, stoking the fire in her slowly, but surely, until she whimpered in his arms, completely spent after the explosive orgasm that she experienced.

But it took Yashodhara just a few minutes after that to get back to her pet subject: Chitrangada's marriage.

"Jeet, do you think you can somehow persuade Raj to come along with us to the function? Please?" She was sitting again, next to him, this time having taken the precaution to don the t-shirt that he had discarded much earlier.

Indrajeet opened one eye to look at his wife. "You haven't given up, have you?"

Yashodhara smiled at him, shrugging. "You know me."

He stacked his hands behind his head, looking up at the ceiling, thinking long and hard. "We can do one thing… and it might just work."

"What?"

He turned and looked into her hazel green eyes with his warm brown ones. "I can plead an important meeting that I simply cannot miss and request Raj to accompany you since you can't go alone in your delicate state of health. What say?"

Yashodhara's face darkened. She did not care for the idea of Indrajeet not going with her to her best friend's engagement. She shook her head now.

"Forget it." She lay down on the bed next to her husband, considering the subject closed.

Sliding down on the bed, he pulled her against him, hugging her close. "No, seriously. Think about it, Yash. The idea has its merits. Anyway, according to you, this engagement is a farce. What does it matter if I don't attend it? Raj will definitely agree to escort you if I plead an urgent appointment that I just cannot miss."

"I don't like it." Yashodhara turned her face into the pillow.

Indrajeet laughed. "No, I can see that. But I can't think of a better idea. Sleep on it and let's talk about it again in the morning."

It was morning and Yashodhara still did not care for the idea of her husband not accompanying her to Chitrangada's engagement. She did not say anything to him about the subject. If Rajvardhan and Chitrangada were meant to meet, they will. There was no need for her to make such a hard effort to bring them together.

It was two days later that Indrajeet spoke on the subject again. "Listen, it looks like I really can't go with you on the thirtieth."

"Why?" Yashodhara looked at her husband suspiciously.

He grinned. "What? You have no trust in me?"

Her gaze softened as she smiled. "You know better than that, Jeet."

"Phew! You had me worried for a moment there," he laughed. "On a serious note, I had been trying to set up an appointment with the minister of agriculture since the past two months. And guess what, they have given me a slot on March 30."

Yashodhara's jaw dropped. "You are serious."

Her husband grinned. "Yep, I am. You know what they say about destiny."

"Are you sure Raj will agree to go with me?" Yashodhara was quite excited at the thought of getting her brother-in-law to meet her best friend. She had a gut feeling that they would get along like a house on fire.

"Leave that to me."

Rajvardhan walked into the dining room as if on cue. "Hey, lovebirds, good morning," he greeted his brother and sister-in-law, giving them a bright smile.

They greeted him in turn, as Ramlal brought another plate from the kitchen.

"Where are the parents?" asked Rajvardhan, piling his plate with a double omelette and three slices of toasted bread.

"Some wedding they had to attend. Listen, Raj. Are you free on the thirtieth?" Indrajeet looked at his brother in enquiry.

"It depends," said Rajvardhan, mischief in his eyes, "how interesting your agenda is."

"Hmm… I can't promise interesting. But there's a need for your services."

"Put that way, I'm all yours. Tell me." Rajvardhan munched his way through the egg and bread even as he spoke to his brother.

Indrajeet gave his wife a lightening glance before looking at his brother. "Yash needs to attend her best friend's engagement at Jodhana."

"The Vasudeva princess?" Rajvardhan looked at his sister-in-law for confirmation.

A surprised Yashodhara nodded at him. He had been listening that day, while she had been convinced that he had been thoroughly distracted. "Yes, that's the one."

"What do you want me to do?"

Indrajeet replied, "I have an important meeting and just can't go with Yash. And I don't want her to go by herself, seeing that she's pregnant."

"I agree. Yasho can't go by herself. I'll go with you, *bhabhi*. No worries. What's this meeting all about?"

The brothers chatted about the upcoming meeting while Yashodhara sat back to enjoy an extra cup of coffee, a smug smile on her face as she surreptitiously crossed her fingers. She just knew that Rajvardhan and Chitrangada were made for each other, unaware that she was but a tool in the hands of Destiny.

11

Chitrangada was on pins the morning of her engagement, not having slept a wink the previous night. While she wanted to scream the place down, she sat down calmly in front of the dressing table, staring at the old, faded photo of her mother's, her eyes pleading with the image for a solution that would get her out of the mess she was in. "Help me, Ma."

Her father had hired an event management agency to take care of the function. By now. Chitrangada did not really care where he got the money to spend on this extravagance. When she had asked him the one time, he had told her that he had saved a nest egg just for such an occasion. "That's what a responsible father does, keep aside a fund for his daughter's wedding. And we are royals. We can't just get away with a shabby affair."

She did not know how irresponsible her father had been; still was. Chitrangada felt bereft in the world, as if she had no one. And she did not want to lose her father too, however he was. The scene when he had threatened to commit suicide kept coming in front of her mind's eye. She did not look at it as a threat but a desperate act on his part. Bikram obviously could not think of a better groom and had promised her hand to Raja Harischandra Gajanan. Now, he did not want to renege on the promise. Well, that she could understand.

But Chitrangada being what she was, could not help looking for a way out. She had run through the whole gamut of ideas. Running away was just not her style. She had thought of persuading her father to sell their property and simply move to another country. But then, she would still be the reason for his early death as she could not see him being uprooted from the Vasudeva palace and lands, whatever was left of them. She thought of pleading that she had some terminal disease. But that sounded so like a loser's idea.

There was no escape, it seemed.

Chitrangada straightened her back. There had to be some way. It was a good thing that her father insisted on the wedding taking place only in September. She planned to hold him to that. It gave her the precious time that she needed to come up with an idea.

Raj's handsome face flashed in front of her eyes. Should she try to meet the Thakore scion and at least find out if he had feelings for her? But she did not want to build on her hopes too much. It may be one solution or it may not. At the end of it all, she had to take care of herself.

One thing the Vasudeva princess was absolutely clear about. She would not let Harischandra Gajanan touch her. No way!

Raja Harischandra Gajanan could not wait for the clock to strike five. The ceremony was set for 6.30 in the evening and he did not want to arrive at the Vasudeva palace too early. He had arrived that morning by his private jet and had checked into a 5-star hotel.

Bhaktavar, his Man Friday, had packed a suit-case that contained three sets of jewellery for his bride-to-be, all set in precious stones that the Raja had imported, set in new designs that he held the copyright to. The three sets were together worth more than five crore rupees. But then, the beautiful princess deserved them all and more. Then, there were the betrothal rings, diamonds set in gold. He had also brought her a dozen silk saris in a myriad of colours.

He could not wait to make her his. Just thinking of her luscious body made him go hard. Getting engaged would definitely give him more rights towards her body. He planned to get as close to her as possible.

For a moment, the flash of revulsion in her eyes came in front of his eyes. Instead of disturbing him, it only made him more excited about making her his. Harischandra gave a mental shrug, sure of overcoming her revulsion with little effort. He would make her sob his name in passion by the end of it all. He was totally confident about it. Why, even the shy Sitara, the first wife he had divorced, had opened up under his expert lovemaking. What the insensitive Raja did not realise was that Sitara had been an innocent who had had just the one agenda, to please her husband—as instructed by her mother—and she had followed it to the T. Her enjoyment had never entered into the equation.

He rubbed his hands in pleasure before lifting the glass of brandy and sipping from it. He was too thrilled with his future. All he needed now was an heir to take forward his lineage.

"You mean the programme is in the evening?" Rajvardhan raised an eyebrow at his sister-in-law fifteen minutes after they were on their way to Jodhana.

"Yes." Yashodhara sincerely hoped that her brother-in-law would not lose his temper.

The friends spoke to each other almost every day. It was only yesterday when Chitrangada had called her to say, "Yasho, will it be possible for you and your husband to come by lunch time? Will Jeet mind terribly? I so need your support."

Chitrangada had sounded kind of distracted on the phone last evening and hence Yashodhara had not bothered to enlighten her that it wasn't her husband, but her brother-in-law who would be accompanying her. And of course, she had agreed to go by lunch.

"Hmm…" Rajvardhan did not say anything, though he wondered how he was going to pass the time at the Vasudeva palace. He supposed that Yashodhara planned to have fun with her friend. But what was he to do there all day long? But he kept his thoughts to himself, not wanting to say anything rude to his sister-in-law in her delicate condition. It was obvious that she was looking forward to spending the day with the Vasudeva princess.

"I'm sorry, Raj. I hope you don't mind. I…"

"It's okay, Yasho." Rajvardhan took his left hand off the steering wheel to pat her on her shoulder. "I have kept myself free the whole day today, so no issues." He gave her a reassuring smile.

Phew! That had been close. She had heard a lot about Rajvardhan's infamous temper, but it looked like he also had an excellent control over it. Yashodhara turned to look out of the window, willing hard that her plan should work.

They reached the Jodhana palace at noon. Rajvardhan stopped the car at the portico and handed the keys to a footman to have it parked.

Just as he took Yashodhara's hand and guided her towards the front door, Chitrangada came rushing out, "Yasho, I'm so happy to see you." Rajvardhan stood there, jolted out of his wits as his Princess hugged his sister-in-law.

The woman he had met in Zurich, the one with whom he had made torrid love over two days and an equal number of nights, the one who had called herself Princess, had a real name now. It was Chitrangada Vasudeva. She also happened to be Yashodhara's best friend. He thought about the conversation he had had with his sister-in-law immediately after his return home. She had suggested an alliance between him and her best friend Princess Vasudeva.

Rajvardhan threw back his head and laughed, startling both women who had been chatting nineteen to a dozen.

Yashodhara grinned at him, finding his laughter infectious, not noticing that her friend had turned pale with shock. "Raj, this is my childhood friend, Princess Chitrangada Vasudeva." She turned to Chitrangada and said, "Chitra, this is Rajvardhan, my brother-in-law. Jeet…" She stopped, noticing the way her friend was staring at her brother-in-law, the colour that had drained from her cheeks, rushing back with a vengeance.

"So, Princess, we meet again." Rajvardhan swept his melting chocolate gaze from the top of her silken head to the tips of her toes, taking his time studying her hour-glass shape and falling in love with her all over again.

"You know each other?" Yashodhara was surprised and more thrilled than ever. This was getting better, it seemed.

Chitrangada nodded her head, hope and despair playing *kabaddi* in her heart, while her stomach roiled as delight and dismay vied for supremacy. Doing her best to keep all emotion under wraps, she said in a casual voice, "Hello, Raj. How have you been?"

"Not too great until this very minute." He turned to his sister-in-law. "Thanks, Yasho, from the bottom of my heart, for bringing me here today. You don't know how much I mean that." He turned back to Chitrangada and said, "So, you were telling me the truth when you said you were getting engaged. Is that why you left without even saying bye?"

"I'll answer you in a minute. Yasho must be tired after the long journey. Let's go in." Chitrangada did not wait for his reply as she took her friend's hand and began walking into the palace.

Rajvardhan walked close to her, whispering in her ear. "Don't even think you are going to get away with it. I need to talk to you and that was like a month ago. You had better make yourself free ASAP."

Chitrangada shivered as she felt his breath on her ear, her whole body delighting in his proximity. Her heart danced with joy. She did not really know how Raj's presence changed the situation. But she already felt lighter. She turned towards him and blew him a kiss, before giving him a slight nod.

No, he was not going to be pacified by that flying kiss. Rajvardhan was too angry with Chitrangada.

She had not just disappeared from his life, she had also taken his heart along with her. And today's meeting was just happenstance. It wasn't as if Princess had made a special effort to contact him.

And he knew for sure that she must have found out all about him on the internet. After all, the snow polo event at St Moritz was searchable on Google. She would have got to know his full name and a lot more details if she had looked for it. Unlike him! Rajvardhan had had no clue who Princess was, not until he set eyes on her just now.

The moment Chitrangada left them alone, Rajvardhan turned to Yashodhara and asked, "Who the hell is she getting engaged to, Yasho? If I remember right, you spoke of an alliance between me and…"

Yashodhara nodded her head vigorously. "You remember right. Chitra is getting engaged to Raja Harischandra Gajanan who…"

Rajvardhan frowned heavily. "What? That old goat? He must be old enough to be her father. I don't get it. Why the hell would she agree to such a match?"

Yashodhara grimaced. "You know him?"

"Not personally, no. But I know enough about him. Do you know that if he weds Princess, she would actually be his third wife?"

Yashodhara was shocked. "What? Are you serious? I just can't understand why Bikram Uncle would want to marry off his only child to such a man."

"Is that Princess Chitrangada's father?" When Yashodhara nodded, he continued, "Forget her father. Why the hell did Princess agree to the alliance? All she had to do was say no." His scowl grew heavier.

"I don't think she was really given a choice, Raj." Yashodhara's words were a whisper now as she saw Chitrangada walking back along with a footman carrying a tray.

Rajvardhan refused to take his eyes off their hostess as he took the proffered cup of coffee, willing her to meet his gaze.

Chitrangada just would not look in his direction, or she might have burst into tears, thinking of what she had left behind in Zurich. Was it too late? She flashed him a glance and noticing his heavy scowl, concluded that Raj must be too angry with her.

Biting into a cookie, Yashodhara said, "I need to make a few calls that are rather urgent. Is there somewhere private where I won't be disturbed?" She turned towards her brother-in-law with a raised eyebrow and was rewarded with a wide smile for her efforts.

"You can use the library." Chitrangada offered in a choked voice, turning to the footman and requesting him to guide their guest to the said room. She got up after that and said, "Would you like to watch TV, Raj? I need to be in the kitchen to check about lunch. I…"

"Not so fast." Rajvardhan snagged her hand in his. "Where's your father?"

"He's out and is expected for lunch." Her voice shook under the impact of his touch.

"Good. Let us go to your room. As I said, I need to talk to you."

"What about, Raj? I… we…"

He took her hand and began to walk towards the staircase, confident that her room must be on the first floor.

Chitrangada went along with him, her heart beating loudly. Over the past few weeks, she had imagined many different ways of meeting Raj again. But she had never thought it would be at her own home, and on the day of her engagement. Hope overpowered despair just now.

By the time they reached the top of the stairs, it was she who was holding his hand in hers as she pulled him along to her room on the right wing. She let go of his hand to open the door and stepped into her room. Rajvardhan walked in right behind her, shutting the door and pushing the bolt in place. He turned to her and pulled her into his arms which were like steel bands that refused to let go. Not that she put up a fight. Chitrangada lifted her face and pressed her lips to his, simply melting in his arms.

This was exactly where she wanted to be!

It was a long while before Rajvardhan lifted his head to look down at his Princess's face. She appeared blissful. "Why, Princess?"

Chitrangada's eyelashes fluttered when she opened her eyes a slit with great reluctance as her eyelids felt too heavy. "Why what?"

"Why did you go away that morning without telling me anything? Without leaving me any way to contact you?" There was pain in Rajvardhan's voice. "I'd throttle you if I didn't want you so much."

Colour rushed up her face as she looked deeply into his eyes. "Did you want to contact me?"

"Don't be an idiot, Princess. Of course, I wanted to get in touch with you. Our lovemaking was explosive, and something that I've never felt before. I thought that you also enjoyed it. Or didn't you?" He looked at her, his gaze shrewd, confident of her answer. He knew for a fact that she had liked it as much, if not more than he had.

She went on tiptoe to take a bite of his sensual lower lip. "You know I did, though I have no experience prior or later to compare it with," she said cheekily.

"Well, that's too bad. You aren't going to get any other experience to compare it with," he said arrogantly, "since you're going to be stuck with me, like forever." If she was not in love with him, he planned to make her fall for him, even if it took him a whole lifetime.

"I wish!"

"Your wish is my command, Princess." Rajvardhan grinned at her, pressing his forehead to hers.

Chitrangada sighed, pulling out of his arms to walk a few feet away, hugging her arms around herself. "I wish life were that easy, Raj."

He walked up to her to hug her from behind, pressing his chin to a slender shoulder. "It's easier than that." His hands caressed her waist before sliding upwards to cup her breasts, squeezing them. "You've lost weight, Princess."

She turned around in a flash and hit him on his chest with a tight fist. "Of course, I have. What do you think? You do remember why you're here today, don't you?"

"Oh yeah, how can I forget? I'm here with my sister-in-law to attend your engagement to a man who's old enough to be your father," he said, his voice heavily sarcastic. "If you think I'm going to let you do it, you need to think again, sweetheart."

Chitrangada shook her head slowly, her shimmering eyes on his as she held back her tears. "And how are you going to stop it, Raj?"

"I'll speak to your father and convince him that I'd make him a better son-in-law. That is, if you will marry me."

She laughed through her tears. "That's some marriage proposal."

"You didn't leave me with a choice, did you?" Rajvardhan growled, his temper flaring. "What would you have done if I hadn't turned up today, Princess? Just gone ahead and got your wedding fixed to that old man, without putting up a fight?"

"Nothing, of course. The same as now. Not a thing has changed, Raj. I'm still going ahead with the engagement."

Rajvardhan placed his hands on her shoulders and shook her hard. "Are you crazy?"

"I suppose I am."

He flung her away from him to turn and walk towards a window, his shoulders slouched in defeat. The way she had kissed him, he had been sure that she had deep feelings for him. But that did not seem so. It looked like Princess only lusted after his body.

His pride came to the fore and Rajvardhan straightened his shoulders before turning to walk towards her. That is when he noticed Chitrangada sitting on her dressing stool, her face buried in her hands, her body shaking with sobs.

"Princess!" Rajvardhan was on his knees beside her the very next moment. "My darling…" He gathered her in his arms. "Talk to me."

She buried her face in his shoulder and howled her heart out. He let her cry, his hand stroking her head gently, waiting for the storm to pass.

Chitrangada calmed down by and by before moving away from him to sit up straight. "I can't escape, Raj. It's my father's life at stake." Her voice was hoarse when she uttered those words.

"Run that by me again; I'm not sure that I heard you right." Rajvardhan gave her a startled look.

She sighed, saying, "If I won't go ahead with this betrothal, my father told me that he'd shoot himself."

"But that's ridiculous."

"Exactly what I would have thought if I were you. But I'm not joking, Raj. He held a gun to his temple and told me he would pull the trigger if I didn't agree to the wedding."

"He really did that? Like he threatened you?" He shook his head in a daze. Why would her father do that? Unless there was way more to this than how it appeared on the surface.

She nodded her head, feeling ashamed of admitting that about her own father.

"Let me understand this correctly. Your father took a real gun in his hand, held it against his head and told you to agree to the wedding or he would kill himself?"

She gave him an impatient look. "That's what I said, just now."

Rajvardhan shook his head again. "I just wanted to cross check that I'd heard you right."

"You did. And that's the reason why I can't get out of today's ceremony."

He nodded, eyeing her keenly, before taking her hand in his. "I love you, Princess. Will you marry me?"

"This isn't a good time to joke, Raj." Chitrangada pouted at him.

He held her dark gaze with his coffee brown eyes even as he pressed his lips to the back of her hand. "Does it seem like I am joking?"

"But, Raj…"

"Answer me, Princess."

"I love you, Raj. But it's too late. I…"

He got up to smother her lips with his own, not letting her complete the sentence. She clung to him, kissing him back with equal passion.

Rajvardhan set her away from him before removing a gold signet ring that had the figure of an elephant with a howdah—the emblem of the Thakores—carved on it, from his little finger. Taking her right hand in his, he slid it on her ring finger. "That makes you mine. And what's mine, stays mine." It was as if he was taking an oath. He lifted her hand to press his lips to the finger on which he had slid the ring.

Chitrangada stared down at her hand that was held in his, the signet ring feeling heavy and unfamiliar on her finger. But it made her feel warm and secure, as if it protected her from all harm. It seemed like her mother had heard her call for help and sent Raj to her. She lifted his hand to press it against her cheek, even as she slid into his arms. "I'm so glad to be yours."

He grinned, giving her a swift kiss before saying, "Let the engagement ceremony take place, since I don't want to push your father into a corner at this juncture. Is there a date for the wedding?"

"Not a date, but yes, they have planned it for September."

"That's a lot of time. I just hope for Gajanan's sake that he doesn't lay a finger on you. I might just kill him, if he tries."

"You almost make me hope that he would try." Chitrangada gave him a wide grin, feeling light after a long time as she threw her arms around his neck and kissed him full on the lips. "I think we should go down. We have left Yasho alone for too long." She let go of him reluctantly, remembering her friend.

Rajvardhan nodded.

They walked back down, a few feet separating them, taking up the pretence of being strangers to each other.

But as they walked in to lunch, Chitrangada could not resist showing off her new ring to her best friend. Yashodhara grinned, hugging her friend before turning to her brother-in-law and saying, "I told you so."

"That you did, Yasho. You're the best. By the way, does Jeet really have an appointment with the agriculture minister today?" he asked, tongue in cheek.

Yashodhara grinned at him, nodding. "He does."

"Well, I just wondered."

All three turned serious when Bikram entered the dining room. Introductions were made and the conversation turned towards the impending function.

Rajvardhan let the others talk as he tucked into his lunch, his eyes studying Raja Bikram Vasudeva surreptitiously, as he wondered what made the man tick.

Why would he threaten his only child to marry a man double her age? And it was not even as if Harischandra Gajanan had a golden heart. He was a blackguard if there was one.

Rajvardhan decided to first find out all about Bikram Vasudeva's angle before setting out to tackle Harischandra Gajanan.

He turned around to see Princess watching him from across the dining table and gave her a sly wink, watching with joy as the colour ran up her cheeks.

Harischandra placed his ring on Princess Chitrangada Vasudeva's left hand, preening like a peacock. He felt confident of owning her now. The only issue now was that she would not look enough at him. She seemed more interested in interacting with the guests and there were plenty of those to distract her. He held her hand in his and refused to let go.

He nodded regally to all those who walked up to the dais to congratulate the two of them, not even taking his hand off from hers to shake the hands of the well-wishers. It was with difficulty that he kept the scowl off his face. How many people had Bikram Vasudeva invited? There were at least a thousand guests. Damn him! It was only an engagement. But again, he also felt good showing off his *fiancée* to the assembled guests, most of whom he knew.

When there was a pause in the long line up of people walking towards them, he lifted Chitrangada's left hand to press his lips to her ring finger.

"May I have my hand, please?" Chitrangada asked her *fiancé*, her voice soft, but firm.

"Yes, maybe once you have kissed mine." Harischandra gave her a flirtatious look.

Chitrangada almost gagged at the bile which rose up into her throat. She flashed a look at Rajvardhan who was seated right there in the front, making sure that she caught his gaze every time she turned towards the guests. Looking at him watching her just now, she blushed, a natural smile appearing on her face. She looked at Harischandra and said, "I don't have your experience, your highness. I am sure you understand that I feel shy." Yes, the rising colour definitely helped to convince the man standing next to her, though her voice was anything but bashful.

Harischandra laughed loudly, a delighted expression on his face as he looked at his *fiancée's* lovely face. It was wonderful to know that today's generation could feel shy too. But the princess must have had a closeted life at the palace. Bikram had mentioned something about her job, but he had not been paying attention. All that would stop once she was his wife, of course. He needed her at his home, full time, giving him all her time and attention.

"Did you see the gifts I brought for you?" He rubbed a finger over the back of her hand, unaware that he was making her skin crawl.

"No, your highness. I'm sorry, but I've really not had the time, what with getting ready for the function and all that. I didn't want to keep you waiting." She laid the butter on thick since that was the plan she and Rajvardhan had come up with, to keep the Raja happy and non-suspicious, until they had a plan in place to oust him.

"That I can well understand. I must say you look beautiful, my dear. Radiant, in fact."

Chitrangada's smile was natural as she recalled why she looked radiant, her eyes going to Rajvardhan once again.

Catching the movement of her eyes as they swept towards the audience for the nth time, Harishchandra turned his head to see who had caught her attention. His face darkened when he saw a handsome man sitting in the front row, next to Princess Yashodhara Jadeja Thakore, and looking steadily in the direction of the dais. Who the hell was he?! Was Chitrangada looking at him repeatedly or just generally in that direction? His blood boiled with jealousy and anger.

He turned to his betrothed and tilting his chin in that direction, asked, "Do you know who's that man sitting next to Princess Yashodhara?"

Chitrangada almost choked. He had noticed. It was all her fault as her eyes had sought Rajvardhan's, once too many times. "That's Yashodhara's brother-in-law, Prince Rajvardhan Thakore," she said, keeping her voice low.

"Where's her husband? Why has her brother-in-law accompanied her?" He lowered his voice to continue, "Do you think she isn't finding her husband's attention enough? I wonder if these two are having an affair on the sly!" He gave her a corner-eyed glance, eager to see her reaction to his accusation.

Chitrangada was not a princess for nothing. While her blood boiled and she felt a powerful urge to slap Harischandra, she kept her rising colour and temper down by sheer will power, looking at the Raja coolly, even managing to give him a smile. "I don't know and to be truthful, I don't care. Yashodhara is a friend and I only wish that she's happy."

Harischandra felt frustrated, his dart not having found its mark. "Can't relate to the modern generation though. I wouldn't let any wife of mine have an affair with another man."

She looked up at him, challenge in her expression as she lifted a shapely brow in question. "I hope the rule applies to the husband too. Or do you think it's okay if the man strays?"

Harischandra lightened up, laughing heartily. It looked like his *fiancée* could be jealous. He threw an arm around her, guffawing loudly. "There's no need to be jealous, my dear. I can't say that I haven't had many affairs. But that's all a thing of the past. I can't wait to make you mine. And talking of that, what do you think of an April wedding?"

Chitrangada didn't miss a beat as she gently slid out of his hold in the guise of feeling shy, replying,

"Come on, Raja Harischandra, you can't deny a woman the privilege of a long engagement. You know, that dreamtime when she conceptualises her wedding, all the ceremonies surrounding it while she contemplates her wonderful future with her handsome husband." She fluttered her eyelashes at him, shamelessly flirting with the man. What did she care? He did not have to know who she was considering getting married to, did he? A soft smile made her face glow, though she kept her gaze away from Rajvardhan with a great effort. That way lay danger.

Harischandra's laughter grew louder. He had to give it to the woman. She had charm and wit. And he realised he could not deny her the time. Well, just six more months. In the meanwhile, he definitely had more license than before. He planned to taste the fare before he owned it. No one could stop him from doing that, not with the cheque of two crore rupees that he had handed to his father-in-law-to-be. He had deliberately made it post-dated by a week, just because it gave him great joy to watch the other man stew.

"You must call me Harry, my dear."

Chitrangada nodded, continuing to smile even though her facial muscles had begun to hurt. "Sure, Harry. And you must call me Chitra." She might just hit him with her heel, if he called her 'my dear' just one more time.

Rajvardhan sat next to his sister-in-law on the left side of the front row, never taking his eyes off Chitrangada on the dais. He had chosen his seat so that she could see him every time she lifted her head to look at the guests.

Chitrangada looked resplendent in a gold-coloured sari, with diamonds on her ears, neck and wrists. With great amusement, Rajvardhan noticed that her hair was piled on top of her head, making her taller than Harischandra by a few inches. He was sure that it was deliberate. He turned to Yashodhara and said, "I'm sure you must have guessed that Princess and I knew each other from before."

She grinned. "It stood out, let's say, about a mile away," she teased.

Colour ran up his rugged cheeks as he gave a nod. "I've caught it bad, I suppose," he grimaced.

"No worse than Chitra." Yashodhara assured him.

"You think so?" He turned his gaze back to her again, as he had been watching his Princess avidly.

"I know so. But that man seems pure evil, Raj. I'm kind of worried." She was careful enough to keep her voice low, not wanting someone to overhear her words.

People walked up to them from time to time, common friends who knew the Vasudevas, the Jadejas and the Thakores, chatting with Yashodhara and Rajvardhan. And everyone wanted to know about the missing Indrajeet too.

Rajvardhan replied to his sister-in-law after the next batch of guests moved on. "Believe me, he is the devil incarnate. But don't you worry, Yasho. I won't let him marry Princess, even if I have to kill him with my bare hands," he growled, glaring at the pair on stage. He wanted to kick Raja Harischandra right at that moment as he had been holding on to Chitrangada's hand since the past ten minutes. Yes, Rajvardhan had been counting the seconds, willing the other man to let go of her hand. But it had not made a difference so far.

Yashodhara looked at his tense face and checked the direction in which he was looking, understanding his ire as she saw Chitrangada's hand in her *fiancé's*. "You know, I can even understand why Harischandra wants to marry her. What I can't understand is why her father would agree to it."

"He has not just agreed to the wedding, Yasho. He has threatened Princess at gun point."

"What?" Yashodhara turned pale with shock. "Are you serious, Raj? Are you saying Chitra's life is in danger?"

He shook his head. "No, not that. Her father threatened to kill himself."

"But that's so strange."

"Exactly what I thought. But now I'm not too sure."

Rajvardhan had been in the library when Harischandra arrived. He had been sitting on a comfortable recliner, reading a book as he had a lot of time to kill, since neither woman—Yashodhara as well as Chitrangada—had wanted him under her feet as they got ready for the function. After a while, he had fallen asleep for some time. Just as he was going to get up, a footman had escorted the Raja into the library where Bikram Vasudeva was seated, waiting for the man. Bikram had obviously not noticed Rajvardhan Thakore. And it did not seem a good idea to reveal his presence just at that moment.

Rajvardhan waited for the right time to make his presence known, only it never came. Bikram and Harischandra greeted each other before the latter handed an envelope to the former. "My part of the contract, Bikram."

"You are truly a gentleman, Harry," Bikram gushed.

"Before you see the content, let me tell you that it's post-dated."

"Oh!" There was a well of disappointment in that single syllable.

"Are you worried?" Harischandra sounded amused.

"No, no, not at all," Bikram laughed sheepishly. "As I said before, you are too much of a gentleman, Harry. Shall we go? It's time to begin the function and the guests have already started arriving."

"Sure, let's go."

Rajvardhan heard a table drawer open and close before a key turned in the lock. He waited a few more minutes before he heard both the men leave the library. It was a good thing that he had not shown himself, it seemed. They had obviously been up to something secretive.

Post-dated! That was what Harischandra had said. That term was generally associated only with a cheque.

If Raja Harischandra had given Chitrangada's father a cheque, did that mean what he thought it meant?

Rajvardhan decided that he would dig deeper, soon.

Just now he continued to speak to Yashodhara. "There's something definitely fishy, Yasho. I think it all boils down to money. Do you have an idea of your friend's financial circumstances? Wait. Don't answer. It's best if we talk on our way back home."

Yashodhara nodded in agreement.

It was past eleven when the Thakores took their leave. Chitrangada tried to persuade the two of them to stay back, but neither was keen. Yashodhara wanted to get back home to her husband while Rajvardhan was not keen to spend the night under the same roof as Chitrangada. He simply did not trust himself to stay away from her.

He had made it a point to take her number and given her his. "I'll be in touch."

Chitrangada waved them off, refusing to feel sad. It was only a matter of time before all her problems would be solved, now that she was not alone in dealing with them.

13

Rajvardhan and Chitrangada chatted into the long hours of the same night. "I've missed you, Princess. You don't know how much. I haven't forgiven you, yet, for the way you just upped and disappeared from my life."

"Mmm… do you plan to take revenge?" She asked, lying against her pillows, a smile on her lips. How she loved him!

"You bet. I'm thinking of many options." Rajvardhan was taking a long walk in the palace garden, never one to sit down while speaking on the phone. He tended to pace whenever he took his cell in his hand.

"Ooh, you're exciting me. I can't wait," she gurgled, shaking with mirth.

"Just wait till I get my hands on you." It felt so good. While he missed her proximity, Rajvardhan was glad to at least be able to hear her voice, chat with her.

"Now that's too tempting. Raj, listen. I want to see you. Can we meet?"

"Are you free tomorrow? We can meet at my farm." He had decided that the next time he met her, he had to have her in his arms.

It was past noon when Chitrangada arrived at Ashvaraj Farms, stopping her car under the portico of the heritage building that was at least a ten-minute drive from the gates of the property.

She got out of the car, pushing her glares to the top of her head as she walked up the half a dozen steps that led to the double doors which lay open. "Raj..." she called hesitantly, taking a step inside the cool hall that was bare of furniture except for a couple of low-slung single sofas with a table in between. These were crowded close to the limestone fireplace with a rough finish. The hall itself was well-lit with long windows on both sides of the main door, with a flooring of white marble.

"Raj!" She raised her voice to call out once again.

"Hey, Princess, you arrived finally." Rajvardhan walked into the house right behind her to throw his arms around her and pull her close to his body. He nuzzled her neck, inhaling deeply of her perfume. "Why did you take so long?"

Chitrangada turned around to bury her face in his shoulder, her arms sliding around his lean waist. "Dad and I got into yet another argument," she said. "I don't want to talk about it. Kiss me!" she commanded.

"With pleasure," he said, lifting her face to his before placing his lips on hers, kissing her thoroughly.

"So, what happened?" He sat down on one of the sofas to pull her down on his lap.

She tugged open a couple of buttons on his shirt before pressing her lips to his chest, not bothering to reply.

"Princess!"

Chitrangada tilted her head to look at him, a shapely eyebrow raised. "Don't you want to make love to me?"

His hand moulded the shape of her bottom as Rajvardhan looked deeply into her eyes. "After you tell me what happened."

"Now. I want you, Raj. I need you to love me, make me forget myself." Her eyes shimmered with unshed tears of frustration. She continued to talk before he could respond, "Between my father and that Harry, they are royally screwing up my life." She gurgled suddenly. "Did I just make a pun?"

Rajvardhan shook his head. "A horrendous one, yeah."

She punched him on his arm with a small fist. "Dad wants me to go visiting at Harry's palace over the next weekend. He tells me that he would go along with me as chaperone." She gave him a bitter smile. "Can you imagine what will happen there?" she asked him rhetorically. "That guy is a lecher if there was one. I swear that a small thing such as not being married would count with him. He's capable of raping me, Raj."

He hugged her close, pressing her face into his shoulder. He could well imagine what would happen if Chitrangada went to stay at Gajanan's palace. It was truly a catch twenty-two situation. "How long can you postpone this trip?"

"A couple of weeks at the max, not longer than that. There's something underfoot, Raj, something that I'm unable to place a finger on. Harry has some kind of a hold over my father. Otherwise, Dad wouldn't be so insistent. I need to get to the bottom of it."

"Er… Princess, I…"

She pushed back against his locked arms to look into his eyes shrewdly. "You know something, don't you? Tell me. I can take it."

"Do you guys have any kind of financial problem?" There was no other way but to ask outright.

Chitrangada frowned. "We aren't very well off. Somehow, Dad keeps landing in debts, don't really know how he manages to do that. He had to sell off our lands. Four hundred acres of them, mind you." She sighed. "We have about a hundred left now. We still have it only because I wouldn't let him sell those too. Can't really understand why he needs so much money. But then, he insisted on a lavish engagement party yesterday, with more than a thousand guests attending. He says that that's the least he could do for his princess." She gave him a bitter smile. "As if I wanted a grand engagement to that bastard."

"Chill, Princess. Temper is not going to sort out our issues. We need to think in a cool frame of mind."

"It's all fine for you to talk, Raj. It's not your head on the block." She glared at him, refusing to calm down.

"Isn't it?" Rajvardhan held her chin firmly as he looked deeply into her charcoal eyes, his chocolate gaze burning a fiery gold.

She fell on his chest, burying her face in it. "I'm sick of it all, Raj. Can't we just turn back the clock and go to that time in Zurich?"

He rubbed a hand down her back in even strokes, trying to calm her down, his mind going around the many ways of getting her out of Harischandra Gajanan's clutches. "Listen, you never did tell me if your father has any financial issues. What does he do?" Rajvardhan knew that Bikram Vasudeva was not yet fifty. What did he do for an occupation?

"Dad manages the farmers, the accounts and all that. Though, to be truthful, I don't know much about what he exactly does. He doesn't like it if I ask too many questions."

"Hmm… now don't blow up and just listen to me. I…"

She sat back on his lap and looked at him with a deep scowl. "What?"

"*Arre*! I haven't even begun telling you. Why don't you sit quietly and listen for a minute?" He paused, lifting a hand to her forehead to smoothen the frown. "You need to calm down, sweetheart, or you might just blow a blood vessel." He pressed his lips to her forehead, hugging her close. "I think Gajanan is paying a dowry for marrying you."

"What?!" Chitrangada jumped off his lap to stand in front of him, her eyes blazing fire. "How dare you, Raj? How dare you say that? I know that Harry is an old goat and I don't want to marry him. But that still doesn't mean that he has to pay money to wed me. How dare you even suggest such a horrid thing?" She began pacing the moment she finished shouting at him, agitated with what she had heard. What if Raj was right? Was her father so crazy as to take money from Harischandra Gajanan? If that were the case, how did Raj know about it when she had no clue?

She stopped suddenly, facing Rajvardhan, bending towards him to place her hands on the arms of the sofa. "How do you know? Or are you just making a wild guess?"

Rajvardhan grimaced. "A bit of both. Princess, is it ever possible to hold a sensible conversation with you?" he asked, his voice impatient as he curbed his quickly rising temper.

"It's my life that's in ruins, damn it!" she snarled at him. She so needed a punching bag and Rajvardhan was available.

"Not yet. But the way in which you are going about it, it's soon going to be." Rajvardhan got up from his seat, taking her hands off the sofa and pushing her away from him. "I'm going to have lunch. You're welcome to join me if you're hungry."

"How can you think of food now?"

"The same way that you can think of having sex. It's a need of the body. So, are you coming?"

"I hate you, Raj."

"And I love you, Princess."

"You are impossible." Chitrangada walked over to him and bunching her fists, hit him on his chest.

Before she could lift them to continue hitting him, he caught both her fists in his hands, moving swiftly to push her against a wall. He bent down to kiss her, his teeth biting into her luscious lower lip, making her moan. Pressing his taut body against her soft one, he continued to kiss her roughly.

Not that Chitrangada protested. She revelled in his passionate kisses, returning them with a matching fervour. "Love me, Raj," she commanded him, a second time.

Lifting her up in his arms without breaking the kiss, Rajvardhan carried her to the back of the hall where he had his bedroom. Dropping her on the bed, he pulled off his shirt and jeans. She stared at him, a greedy expression on her face as she watched first the magnificent chest and then the muscular legs that came into view. "Ooh! But you're simply gorgeous."

"Aren't you getting naked?" he asked, pulling her into his arms.

"Do you wanna undress me?" she asked, fluttering her eyelashes at him.

"I might have, if I could manage it. Look at my hands," he said, offering them for her view. They were trembling. "I'm dying to mate with you, Princess."

"Oh, you poor baby! And here, I've been arguing with you non-stop." Chitrangada pulled off her t-shirt and threw it away, peeling her skinny jeans immediately after. Just as she was removing the catch on her bra, she felt herself falling on the bed as Rajvardhan pushed her back. She threw her arms around him, lifting her head to capture his mouth with her own, tangling her tongue with his.

His hands cupped her breasts, kneading their plumpness, his lips tracing the shape of her throat, stroking her pulse points with his tongue. Chitrangada's head fell back on the soft pillows as she let him have his way with her. She giggled when he nibbled her collar bone, his lips moving inadvertently down towards her aching breasts. While his touch felt wonderful, she could not wait to have his mouth on them. "Please Raj," she begged him.

He lifted his head to give her a naughty look, "Please what?"

"I want your mouth on my breasts. It has been so long. Please love me, now, before I die."

"Dramatic, aren't we!" He laughed softly before taking a swollen tip into his warm mouth.

She held his head in both her hands, pushing her body closer to him, making mewling noises from the depth of her throat. "Yes, yes," she moaned, "give me more."

After pleasuring her breasts to their mutual satisfaction, he moved down, his lips fluttering over her abdomen, making her tremble with desire as his tongue swirled around her navel, even as his hand cupped her femininity.

She clutched his shoulders, her nails digging into them as she almost jumped off the bed in her eagerness to be taken.

"I've missed you, Princess." Rajvardhan declared, as he plunged himself into her body with a groan.

"Not more than I have missed you, Raj. Don't stop," she moaned, her legs locked tightly around his waist, urging him to take her.

"Never, my sweetheart," he said, riding her hard. They reached their climax as one before Rajvardhan fell on her, thoroughly spent.

It was another hour before they finally got to the dining table where Suruchi set forth steaming bowls of food. She was foreman Kanhaiya's wife and cooked at the main house whenever Rajvardhan and his family visited the place. "They live in a cottage on the farm," said Rajvardhan, filling a plate with *laal maas* and *aloo gobhi*, adding two hot *naans* dripping with ghee that were straight out of the clay oven built in the open space behind the kitchen, before handing it to her. Suruchi walked back and forth as she brought fresh *naans* to the table.

When they were more than halfway through lunch, Rajvardhan said, "I suppose you've calmed down enough to have a decent dialogue now," running a roving eye over Chitrangada, who still appeared a bit dishevelled due to their earlier lovemaking, even though she had done her darnedest to make herself presentable. Liking what he saw, he grinned at her, before closing one eye in a sly wink.

Hot colour steamed her cheeks as she stared right back at him, her gaze clinging to his. He was a terrific lover and their riotous lovemaking had calmed her down like nothing else could. She eyed Suruchi from the corner of her eyes when the cook brought some more hot breads to the table. "Thanks, Suruchi. I can't eat any more." Chitrangada stopped the other woman from serving her another *naan*.

"I have had enough too, Suruchi. The food was excellent," said Rajvardhan. "You go off now to have your lunch with Kanhaiya. I'll clear up here."

"No, no, *Kunwarji*. Allow me…"

"Go now. It's way past your lunch time. If you want, I'll leave the table as it is. You can come back later to clear it up."

"*Ji!*" Suruchi suddenly seemed to realise that the royal couple wanted to be left alone. She almost ran out of the backdoor, Rajvardhan's soft laugh following her.

"You still haven't told me if your father's facing any financial issues."

"None that I know of." Chitrangada's lips drooped as she thought about how secretive her father really was. "I've been earning my keep since the past few years." She was actually thinking aloud, running her thoughts by him. "I know for a fact that the kitchen is run off the provisions and veggies from the farm. Even the fruits come from the orchards that we have. For all other expenses," she frowned, thinking hard, "I think Dad has some cash reserve." She glared at Rajvardhan. "He must have, right? Or he wouldn't have spent so many lakhs on the stupid engagement party."

He raised both hands in a gesture of peace, his eyes gentle. "Don't take off like a rocket once again. I swear I have nothing to do with all this. I'm just trying to understand the basics here."

"As if it's any of your business," Chitrangada muttered under her breath, her smile of before having disappeared completely.

"I wonder if it's best to just tie you to a bed and make love to you all the time? That might just about keep you in good humour," he asked lazily, a dark eyebrow rising up to touch his hairline. "Or maybe I should just put you across my knees and give you the spanking that you so richly deserve."

"You wouldn't dare." Instead of anger, Chitrangada felt a flare of excitement as she looked into his coffee brown eyes.

"Wouldn't I?!" Rajvardhan got up from his chair with a purposeful expression on his face.

"Raj!" She squealed as he approached her, not moving an inch.

He walked over to her and lifted her in his arms, carrying her out of the dining room.

"Put me down, Raj." She clung to him, her arms around his neck, rejoicing in his hold, a shiver of desire dancing down her spine.

Without listening to her, he carried her out through the front door.

"Where are you taking me?"

"I'm planning to dunk you in the lake." He paused in his stride to answer her.

"Let me go, you brute." She fought to get out of his arms, only to find that they had turned into steel bands as they tightened around her.

"Either that, or I spank you. You're letting your temper get the better of you, Princess. I have satisfied your cravings, for both food and sex. But you still…"

"Shut up, Raj. You're being crude." She kicked him on his shin, only to yowl in pain as she hurt her toes badly while he stood there grinning down at her.

Rajvardhan gave an exaggerated sigh, removing his arms from around her. "Go away then. I'll deal with the problem in my own way. I don't need your help."

"What?!" Chitrangada stood rooted to the spot, startled by his words. He could not be meaning to send her away. They still had not hit upon a strategy to stop her wedding to Harischandra. "But we haven't yet come up with a plan."

"And how do we get to do it? You are too hot-headed, Princess. And planning requires cool thinking. I think it's best that you leave now and allow me to deal with the situation." He turned away from her, beginning to walk towards the house.

Chitrangada ran behind him, catching up with his long strides, tucking her hand into his big one. "I'm sorry," she said in a whisper, pressing her lips to his ear. "I've truly tried your patience today. I can see that. Forgive me?"

Rajvardhan stopped in his tracks to look down at her, his frown melting away the moment he set eyes on her lovely face. He just could not remain angry with his Princess, not for long. He gathered her in his arms and kissed her softly. "You lead me a fine dance, woman."

Chitrangada gurgled with laughter, pleased to hear his words, taking it for the compliment that it was. "So, tell me, why do you think that my dad's taking dowry from Harischandra?"

Rajvardhan told her about the envelope that her *fiancé* had handed over to her father just before the engagement. "Gajanan said that it's post-dated and your father sounded disappointed."

"Oh! Post-dated means he must have been talking about a cheque."

"Exactly the conclusion I arrived at. What I have been thinking is that…" He told her about the plan he had. Chitrangada listened to him, without interrupting, agreeing with him even while offering her thoughts on it.

It was six o' clock when she realised that it was time to leave. "I don't want to go, Raj." Chitrangada protested, continuing to sit on his lap, reluctant to leave his arms.

"We'll be married by end of April," he said, out of the blue.

She squealed in delight. "Is that a promise?"

"Yes."

14

"Raj…" Chitrangada's voice shook when she spoke to Rajvardhan on the phone. "I managed to check Dad's desk, Raj." She stopped to take a deep breath, smothered by the feeling of hurt, the likes of which she had never felt before. "There's this cheque for two crore rupees that is post-dated April 6. That's probably the one they had been talking about on the day of the engagement."

"Shit!" Rajvardhan wished that he were at hand to hold his heart-broken Princess in his arms. She sounded so forlorn, so unlike herself. "Sweetheart…"

"Raj, can you believe it? It looks like my father has sold me to the highest bidder." Her voice was bitter as Chitrangada stared vacantly at the wall in her bedroom, where she had incarcerated herself before calling Rajvardhan.

"I am coming over." He could not take the pain in her voice. "I suppose you're at home?"

"Yes. But, Raj…"

"Don't go anywhere. I'll see you as soon as I can. Where's your father?"

"He should be home for lunch in half an hour."

"Good. I need to talk to him too."

"No, Raj. I don't think it makes sense. He won't…"

"I'll see about that." What Rajvardhan had not told Chitrangada yet was that the detective he had hired—Samrat—had already uncovered a lot of things about Bikram Vasudeva. The Raja of Jodhana was an inveterate gambler. And like all gamblers, he had only lost money in the long run, never making any. Hence the desperate selling of four hundred acres of land which had been in the Vasudeva family since a little less than five hundred years. He had agreed to Harischandra's offer for Chitrangada's hand in return for five crore rupees. Out of the first crore he had received, Bikram had managed to pay off his debtors to the tune of seventy lakhs. And he had managed to keep all this away from his daughter. It was time to have a talk with Chitrangada's father.

"Listen to me, Raj…" But Chitrangada was talking in the air as her call had been disconnected.

She turned and buried her face in the pillow, her eyes burning. She was too upset to even cry. And when had tears solved anything? She suddenly banged a tight fist on the bed. Why? Why had her father done this to her? He loved her, didn't he? He professed to have remained unmarried after Chitrangada's mother's death so that she would not have to face an evil stepmother. What had happened to all that love?

Her stomach churned in anxiety. The threat of marriage to Harischandra had taken a backseat in the face of her father's betrayal. Why did he need so much money?

She sat up with a jerk, bringing her knees close to her chest and wrapping her arms around them. Her chin pressed to her knees, she traced a pattern on the bedsheet, her gaze unseeing. Raj was coming. But what would he do? *What could he do?* Can he make her father love her? A drop of tear appeared in the corner of her left eye before rolling down her cheek. Chitrangada lifted a hand to rub her face, wiping it away angrily, only to have another one rolling right behind.

And she was suddenly flooded with grief, just like that, as she mourned the death of her relationship with her father, the end of his love for her. But then, had he loved her, ever? What kind of love would want his young daughter to get married to an old man, that too as a third wife?

In a fit of temper, Chitrangada lifted the brass lamp that was on her bedside table and threw it across the room, where it broke into three pieces, each one rolling away in a different direction.

"Princess!" Rajvardhan had been climbing the staircase to the first floor when he heard the noise of something breaking. He ran across the corridor and rushed into her room. "Sweetheart!"

Chitrangada flew into his arms, hugging him tight. "Take me away from here, Raj. I don't want to live here anymore. I hate my father."

He held her close to his heart, not uttering a word as she ranted and raved, heaving abuse on her father. He kept his silence while he waited for all the poison to drain out of her system. It was a long while before Chitrangada calmed down, her breath coming in hiccups.

She moved away from him, or at least tried to. He would not let her go. "I'm sorry, Raj. I must seem like a shrew. I hope you don't hate me by now." She lifted her face to his, a pathetic expression on her face.

Rajvardhan lifted a hand to brush back the curls tumbling all over her face, before cupping her cheek. "You know something? I like the spirited woman any day more than the one who's lacking in confidence. You are a fighter, my darling. Don't ever change."

Her eyes went wide on hearing his words. "You still think I have it in me, Raj? I feel lost just now, as if the fight has left me, forever."

He hugged her close. "Believe me, your spirit's just gone on a short break. It'll be back sooner than you think." He lifted her chin to look into her face. "That was the first thing that I fell in love with you about, your fighter spirit that makes you the queen of my heart."

A small sliver of a smile broke out on her face, like a tiny ray of sunshine after a dark and heavy storm. "Are you saying you still love me after my tantrum?" She shook her head at him. "You must be crazy."

"Of course, I am. About you." He bent down to give her a swift kiss on her lips, before giving her a playful slap on her bottom. "Let's go talk to your father."

"In a minute." Chitrangada pressed closer to him, kissing him on his lips, stroking her tongue over his mouth. "I can't wait to be yours."

"That, you already are, my Princess. No one can take you from me."

They left her bedroom, hand-in-hand, to beard the lion in its den.

"Dad, I'm glad to see that you are home." Chitrangada felt choked as she tried her best to instil some enthusiasm into her voice as she spoke to her father.

"Yes, my child. Shall we go to lunch?" Bikram got up from where he had been sitting on the chair behind his antique desk, nursing a balloon glass containing brandy, honey, and hot water.

"Sure, Dad. And see who's here."

Bikram Vasudeva frowned when he noticed Rajvardhan Thakore, who had walked in behind his daughter. "Prince Rajvardhan Thakore, welcome." He shook the younger man's hand, the frown still on his face. He did not like the Thakore scion visiting his daughter. Damn it! Chitrangada was an engaged woman. And Bikram, more than anyone else, knew how difficult it had been to convince her to get betrothed to Raja Harischandra Gajanan. It would not do anyone any good for a young and handsome bachelor to visit her. The temptation might just be too much for his daughter.

"Hello, Bikram Uncle. I need to talk to you."

"Shall we have lunch first?" Chitrangada asked solicitously, postponing the inevitable, not looking forward to what was to unfold.

Bikram looked from one to the other, wondering about Rajvardhan's visit. What did the man want? Why did he need to talk to him? He got up from his chair and said, "Yes, let's have lunch first."

It was more than an hour before the three of them settled down in the library, on the comfortably deep sofas that were strategically strewn around to give an impression of casual relaxation.

"Tell me, what do you need to talk to me about?" There was no smile on his face when Bikram addressed their unexpected guest.

"Er… Uncle, I know you might think that it's none of my business. But…"

"Dad, why did Harischandra give you a cheque for two crores?" Chitrangada blurted out, unable to control herself. Her face had a pinched look when she looked directly at her father.

"What?!" Bikram Vasudeva got up with a jerk, his teacup falling out of his hands and rolling on the floor, the leftover tea leaving brown marks on the cream carpet. "How dare you, Chitra? How dare you question your father? That too, in the presence of a stranger?" He glared at his daughter, fury in his eyes, before turning his gaze to Rajvardhan. "I think you should leave, Prince Thakore."

"No!" Chitrangada's voice was a scream.

"I'm going nowhere, Raja Bikram. I did tell you that I needed to talk to you."

"Do you want me to get my men to throw you out?" Bikram threatened the younger man.

Rajvardhan gave him a mirthless smile. "Do you really think that's possible? Sit down, Raja Bikram. I probably have a solution to your problems. Why don't you just hear me out?"

"But who said that I have a problem? I don't need your help. Just get out." Bikram fisted his hands in frustration. If he had been twenty years younger, he would have bodily thrown the other man out of his home, or at least would have tried to. But he had not only aged, but had also let his body go to fat, completely unfit. His sedentary lifestyle of playing cards at different clubs for most of his waking hours had surely not helped him stay fit.

Rajvardhan looked at Chitrangada before turning towards her father, hoping that she would not kill him for what he was going to tell Bikram Vasudeva. "Raja Bikram, I know that you are a gambler and have been one for the last twenty-five years. And through all those years, you have only lost money, never gained a rupee."

Bikram Vasudeva sat down on the sofa with a thud. "What the hell do you mean?" But there was no strength in those insulting words, even as he turned to look at his stricken daughter. "He's lying, Chitra."

Chitrangada had been staring at Rajvardhan with accusing eyes, only to turn to her father when she heard

Bikram's response. She went pale when she saw the guilty colour on her father's face. "Dad…" she called out, her voice a hoarse whisper, "you know that Raj is telling the truth." She bit her lip hard. She would not cry. She had shed enough tears that morning, enough to last her a lifetime.

Bikram looked at both of them, a pathetic expression on his florid face. "How did you find out?"

Rajvardhan sighed, not really enjoying what he was doing. But it had to be done, for the sake of his Princess. "Does it matter, Uncle? Suffice to say that I know. How much do you owe your debtors?"

Bikram shook his head. "I don't owe any money to anyone." His voice was defiant, though he was fast regaining confidence in the fact that he could be truthful about not having debts any longer.

"How did you manage to pay your latest debts?"

"Who the hell are you to question me?"

"Rajvardhan Thakore is the man I'm going to marry, Dad." Chitrangada's voice was firm when she addressed her father.

"I refuse to believe this nonsense, Chitra. You are engaged to wed Raja Harischandra Gajanan, not this upstart. I beg your pardon, Prince Thakore," he said sarcastically, turning to glance at Rajvardhan with baleful eyes.

She continued to speak, ignoring her father's words, "Raj is questioning you to only help us. If you don't want to answer him, I think we'll leave you immediately, to live your life exactly the way you want to. And," she continued after a pause, "don't try threatening me with a gun to your temple. I'm not scared anymore. If you love me so less that you don't have any qualms about selling me off to Harischandra Gajanan, do you think I really care what you do?" Her voice almost broke before she managed to hold herself together, drawing strength from Rajvardhan's hand on hers.

Shaken, Bikram stared at his daughter. "Do you really think that I am so bad, Chitra?" His voice broke as the magnanimity of the situation struck him. His mind worked fast, thinking of ways to buy time. It was not as if he was feeling any kind of remorse about selling his daughter to Gajanan. His main worry was that if Chitrangada disappeared, Gajanan would definitely come after her father. He could see his recently acquired life of luxury falling apart before his very eyes.

"Worse, Dad." She turned her face away from him.

"I think we can still salvage the situation." Rajvardhan spoke, breaking the silence that had followed the dialogue between father and daughter.

"How?" Bikram's voice was a trembling with angst. "You don't know Harischandra Gajanan. He will kill us all."

Rajvardhan laughed softly. "You don't know *me*, Raja Bikram. I can deal with the likes of Gajanan with one hand tied behind my back. But before all that, I need to know the whole truth about your financial status and all your dealings with the man." His expression was stern when he addressed Chitrangada's father.

Bikram Vasudeva sat up straight, wiping all the expression from his face. "I don't think it's any of your damned business." No, he did not want a change in the status quo.

"I'm not sorry to inform you that it is. Right now, it might seem as if Chitrangada doesn't care what happens to you. But I am sure she will realise soon that we don't want your blood on our hands. And you are right in thinking that Gajanan will kill you for sure, once he realises that his *fiancée* has flown the coop." Rajvardhan did not mince his words. "I think the only way forward is for you to co-operate. Think about it, Raja Bikram. I will," he looked at the silver watch on his left wrist, "give you fifteen minutes."

Raja Bikram Vasudeva fretted and fumed, then ranted and raved over the next ten minutes. It finally struck him that his daughter was not going to budge in her decision as she sat across him on a single sofa, her arms folded tightly across her chest, an angry expression in her dark eyes that so reminded him of her mother, his late wife, Chandrika.

The next five minutes, his mind thought of the many ways to escape the situation. He was not keen at all to return the cheque that he had received from Raja Harischandra Gajanan. And how the hell could he pay back the first one crore that he had already cashed? Most of that money had gone to pay his debts.

Prince Rajvardhan Thakore was being ridiculous. What kind of solution could he bring to this situation?

But then, looking at the determined expression in Chitrangada's eyes, it was obvious that she was ready to walk out of their home. Once she was gone, Gajanan would definitely murder him. There was no escape from that one. It had been a mistake leaving such a long gap between the engagement and the wedding. Bikram sighed loudly. It had all been his mistake. He had thought that a long engagement would give his daughter time to adjust to the idea of marriage and also give her an opportunity to get to know her *fiancé*. But the girl had turned out to be a traitor. His chest heaved with the strong emotions churning inside him. He had given his whole life to take care of her, had showered her with so much love and attention and this is what he got in return.

He looked up to glare at Rajvardhan Thakore. Stud! That is what he was. No wonder he had turned his daughter's head. To his knowledge, they had only met during the engagement, which had been just two days ago. How did they get to the point of wanting to marry each other?

It was twenty minutes before Bikram opened his mouth. "What do you suggest, Prince Thakore?" His voice was polite, not betraying his thoughts. He had decided to pretend to go with Thakore's idea. It was best to take Raja Harischandra Gajanan into his confidence. That was the only way to bring his daughter under control.

"Phew! Thank you, Dad." Chitrangada gave her father a relieved smile.

Rajvardhan was not so easily convinced of the older man's capitulation. For one thing, Bikram still looked unhappy and the prince did not miss the calculating expression in his eyes. All his senses on alert, Rajvardhan said, "Raja Bikram, if you could tell me the amount of your latest debts, I'll help you pay them off."

"They are already paid off. I told you that." Bikram gave Rajvardhan a mocking glance, as if he was talking to a half-wit.

"That money has been paid with what you received from Gajanan, right? You…"

"Dad," Chitrangada interrupted, shock in her eyes, "have you taken more than these two crores?"

Bikram looked from one to the other, hatred in his eyes. "What do I do, Chitra? The debtors were getting restless. You know how some of these goons are."

Chitrangada shook her head at him. "Why, Dad? Why keep gambling when you have been losing so much all these years? I believed you had sold the lands for the upkeep of our palace and for a luxurious lifestyle." Her lips drooped.

"You won't understand, Chitra. You never will. Your mother didn't either. Women are such fools," declared Bikram bitterly. "They don't understand the needs of a man."

"You are right. I don't." Chitrangada's voice was vehement.

"Sorry to interrupt, Raja Bikram, but to get the conversation on track, how much money did you originally take from Gajanan?

Not seeing a way out, Bikram replied, "One crore."

Chitrangada hid her face in her hands, unable to look at her father or at Rajvardhan for that matter. She felt sick and ashamed.

"Give me your bank details and let me transfer one crore rupees into your account. Please return the money to Gajanan and also this cheque." Rajvardhan's voice was authoritative.

"I am not a beggar. I don't need your alms." Bikram was shouting by now.

Rajvardhan gave the other man a stern look. "I'm not used to giving alms to the tune of a crore, Raja Bikram. That kind of money rolling happens only in royal households. I am giving you this money only for one reason. It's because you happen to be the father of the woman I love more than my life."

Father and daughter stared at the prince, identical gasps on their lips, though for entirely different reasons.

Bikram gave him a sly look. He will take the money for now. But he needed to somehow convince them that Chitrangada had to visit her *fiancé* over the next weekend, along with her father. He must tell Raja Harischandra Gajanan to organise the wedding on the same weekend. He had no plans to give up five crores for the measly one crore that Prince Thakore had offered.

"Okay, Thakore." Bikram got up from his seat, making it obvious that the meeting was over. "I'll get Chitra to send you the details immediately. But on one condition. I need to take her to Gajanan's home for a weekend. That's something we cannot escape. I will return all his money right then and also get the engagement cancelled. I am sure both of you will agree to this."

Chitrangada nodded her head vigorously, a relieved smile on her face as she ran to her father to give him a hug. "Thank you so much, Dad. I love you!"

Rajvardhan stared at the older man, a shrewd look on his face. His gut instinct was not to believe Raja Bikram's words. He decided to keep his opinion to himself, not wanting Chitrangada to be unhappier than what she had been from morning.

"I'll take your leave then, Raja Bikram. I will transfer the amount to your bank the moment I get the details."

"Wait, Raj. I'll see you out."

Chitrangada walked out of the library with Rajvardhan's hand in hers, only to stop in the entrance hall to kiss him deeply. "I love you, Raj."

"I love you too, my Princess. I have a condition though."

"Anything. Tell me." She gave him a wide grin, feeling so light and happy.

"I plan to be part of your entourage when you visit Gajanan's home." He lifted a hand to stop her protest,

"I'm not taking no for an answer. And, promise me that you will not mention this to a living soul."

Her expression fell. "You don't trust Dad."

"If you want me to tell you the truth, then no, I don't."

"I hate you, Raj."

"I would rather you hate me than get hurt, sweetheart. I'll be seeing you soon." He bent down to give her a swift, hard kiss before stepping out of the Vasudeva palace.

Over that week, Rajvardhan went to visit two people, the names given to him by Samrat, the private detective. Firstly, he went to Mandvi, on the coast of Kutch in Gujarat, to meet Princess Sitara Gaekwad, ex-wife of Harischandra Gajanan. He had taken a prior appointment through her social secretary and landed on their private landing pad by helicopter.

Rituraj, the secretary with whom he had spoken, had brought a car to the helipad to receive him.

"Welcome to the Gaekwad Palace, Prince Rajvardhan Thakore." Rituraj greeted the guest with folded hands.

"Thank you, Rituraj."

The ride to the palace took them barely five minutes and Rajvardhan was shown into a sitting room that was to the right of the main hall of the palace. Taking in his opulent surroundings, Rajvardhan walked along with Rituraj and settled down in a corner of a long and low-slung sofa.

"Princess Sitara should be with you in a minute," said Rituraj. "In the meanwhile, may I get you something to drink? Would you like some coffee or tea or maybe something stronger?"

"Coffee should be fine." Rajvardhan did not think it was a good idea to drink along with the princess. Though he did not know her personally, he had heard a bit about her before he got a whole dossier of information that Samrat had put together on her. Princess Sitara was a recluse who immersed herself in social work. She headed many charities and preferred to keep her work quiet.

He stood up when she walked in just then. Tall and slim to a fault, the princess was clad in an ivory coloured, crepe silk sari, three ropes of translucent pearls decorating her slender neck. If he had not known for a fact that she was thirty-four, he would have thought that she was in her mid-twenties. Her face was unlined with minimal make-up while her hair was tied back in a low knot at the back of her neck. Talk about understated elegance!

"Hello, Princess Sitara," he greeted when the secretary made the introduction.

She looked at him with piercing grey eyes as she responded, "Hello, Prince Rajvardhan, welcome to my home. Please sit down. Rituraj, have you sent for something? What would you like to have, Prince Rajvardhan?" Though soft, her voice was commanding.

A footman walked in just then with a heavily laden tray and placed it in front of Sitara. She sent him on his way with a flick of her wrist before pouring the fragrant coffee into two silver cups. Rituraj followed the footman, excusing himself.

She looked at her guest enquiringly before adding cream and sugar to both cups. She offered a cup and saucer to him along with a tiny silver spoon. "Here you go."

When they sat back to relish their coffee, Rajvardhan said, "I'm so glad that you could meet me at such short notice, Princess Sitara. And as I mentioned on the phone, the matter is urgent." He briefly told her about her ex-husband's engagement to Chitrangada; how Gajanan had managed to trap Bikram Vasudeva into agreeing to the alliance. "It's like this, Princess Sitara. Harischandra Gajanan is a snake. It won't be enough just to return his money. He will not let go of Princess Chitrangada for just that. What I am planning is to create a strong enough case against the man. I'm…"

"Why are you telling me all this?" Sitara pinned her guest with her sharp gaze, without any expression on her face.

"Well, Princess Sitara, you used to be married to Raja Gajanan. That's why…"

She gave an incredulous laugh. "But that was, let me see, eighteen years ago. And I had been married to him for less than two years. What do you think I can do about the present situation?"

"If I've heard right, you do a lot of philanthropic work, don't you?" he asked, taking off at a tangent.

She gave him a regal nod. "So?"

"Couldn't you consider this one more such work? Chitrangada and I love each other and want to get married. It will take me but a minute to take her away and marry her. But," he paused and looked into her eyes, waiting for his words to sink in before continuing, "Gajanan is even capable of murdering her father. Simply returning his money isn't going to pacify him. He won't let Raja Bikram Vasudeva renege on his promise. I'm sure you understand that." It was Rajvardhan's turn to pin her with his piercing brown gaze that had not missed the way she winced on hearing the word 'murder'. He sat back on the sofa after pouring himself a second cup of coffee, relaxed now that he had gotten under her skin. Now, he just had to wait for her to talk. He was confident that she would.

Sitara eyed the man in front of her and could see that he was being completely honest. Immediately after giving him an appointment, Rituraj had put together a file load of information about Prince Rajvardhan Thakore and handed it to her to study. Not keen to read the whole file, she had run through the highlights that had been typed out on one sheet of paper. She had heard about the Thakores of Udaipur, of course. Reading through the sheet, she had realised that the family was as honest as they came. She sighed now, wishing, though uselessly, that she had had access to all information about her ex-husband, before they had tied the knot. But then, if that had been the case, her parents would have never got her married to Raja Harischandra Gajanan.

"Tell me, what do you want to know?"

"Thank you," said Rajvardhan. "You were married to Raja Gajanan for less than two years. May I ask you why you got divorced?"

She gave him a smile that did not really reach her eyes. "I suppose that happened because of my lucky stars. To tell you the truth," she turned her gaze away to stare at the wall behind him sightlessly, "those twenty-two months were the worst period of my life. If I say that Harry is an animal, I would actually be insulting animals. He's a monster and a sadist. He gets a kick out of others' pain." Her voice was dry and expressionless as she told him this.

"Er… Princess…"

She raised a hand to stop him from talking. "Let me finish everything at one go." She looked at him then. "I hope what I am saying just stays with you." She continued when he nodded, "I needed many sittings of therapy to come out of the trauma that was my marriage. I was barely sixteen when I got married to him. My agenda was only to keep him happy. I accepted every kind of cruelty that came my way. He's a sexual pervert if there's one." She had gone back to staring at the wall behind him. "Beating me up for the fun of it was an everyday incident. This continued for a year and a half and suddenly one fine day he wanted to find out why I wasn't getting pregnant. I don't really know what the doctor had told him, but he stopped being violent and even tried to be nice to me in his own style." She shuddered at that point, but continued to talk in a steady voice, "After a couple of more months, I was admitted to a maternity nursing home where a battery of tests was conducted on me." Her eyes moved forward to meet his as a soft laugh escaped her throat. "You know something, Harry thinks that everyone is an idiot and he's the only intelligent person on earth. He wasn't aware or bothered that I could read and write. The reports said clearly that there was nothing wrong with me. But he spread the word around that I was barren. Harry hit the doctor who suggested that he should take some tests too. It would have been hilarious if it hadn't been pathetic. But then, didn't I say that my stars were lucky? That was my ticket to freedom, that I couldn't get pregnant with his child, due to no fault of mine."

"Did you go to the police? Didn't your parents have anything to say about it?"

"My parents were terribly upset. Until the time they passed on, they were sad that I was single and not happily married. They missed having grandchildren." She shuddered again. "Never again. Never will I let someone have that kind of power over me again. And to answer your question, we didn't go to the police. For one thing, Harry is pure evil and we didn't want him creating more trouble for us. For another, as I mentioned earlier, I had just had a lucky escape. Why would I go to the police?"

"But, Princess Sitara, isn't it only fair that the world knows what a blackguard Gajanan is? By keeping quiet, haven't you allowed him to go scot-free and let him continue to harass other women? Do you know that Gajanan had married a second time?"

Princess Sitara gave a small nod, her mind working furiously. Was he right? Had she made a mistake in keeping quiet about her troublesome marriage? At the time of divorce, she had been completely shattered. So much so that it had taken her a very long time to realise that she was finally free of the demon that she had been married to. The need to care for her had what had kept her parents going or they might have simply died of shock. None of them had really thought of making the information public. All said and done, it was not something one felt proud about and wanted to share with others.

"I heard about it."

"Did you know that his second wife was murdered?"

"What?" Sitara's eyes rounded in shock as she looked up at him, stunned. "Murdered? You mean Harry actually murdered his wife?" She shut her eyes, taking deep breaths to calm down her thundering heart, before opening them again. "That could have been me." Her voice was a soft whisper now.

"Exactly! That's exactly what I meant when I said that you should have exposed Gajanan for the monster he is."

"But how would I do that? Who would listen to me? He has so much power, such clout over so many people. A number of politicians and policemen eat out of his hand. What sense would it make to go against him?"

Rajvardhan nodded. "You are right, Princess Sitara. I just need one help from you. You don't need to go public. I just want you to talk about your experience in front of a magistrate and that it goes into record. This information will not be made public. It's only to get an arrest warrant against Gajanan."

"After all these years? Do you think it's possible?"

"With just your testimony, no. Your words will be only one part of the case I am putting together against Raja Gajanan. There will be more. But, as someone who has suffered his cruelty, your statement will be of great help in helping other hapless women. I am there for Princess Chitrangada and she will escape. But there are bound to be other women who will continue to suffer at Gajanan's hands."

"You are right, Prince Rajvardhan. I never realised that my silence is probably the cause of many other women suffering at Harry's hands. That's so terrible, and I feel responsible for that woman's murder." There was remorse in Sitara's voice.

"I hope you won't beat yourself about it. You were only a teenager when you were divorced. And you had to pick up the pieces of your life. You…"

Sitara sighed. "Well, not directly responsible for her death. But… anyway, that's all water under the bridge. What should I do now? I will give my testimony against Harry most definitely."

"Thank you, Princess Sitara. That's truly big of you." Rajvardhan got to his feet. "I'll take your leave now. Let me get an appointment and call Rituraj."

"Sure, Prince Rajvardhan. I'm glad to have the opportunity to atone."

Rajvardhan took her leave, touched by her magnanimity. She was the injured party and she was talking about atonement. Princess Sitara was truly a great woman. He was all admiration for her.

After confirming Sitara Gaekwad's co-operation, Rajvardhan went to Indore the very next day. He flew over on a commercial flight, to be met by Samrat at the Devi Ahilya Bai Holkar airport at 11 am.

"Hello, Samrat, how's it going?"

"All well, Prince Rajvardhan," said Samrat, a smile on his face as they shook hands.

"You must call me Raj. I don't like to stand on formality."

"Sure, Raj."

They got into the car that Samrat had hired for the day. The private detective drove them over to a small hotel in the heart of the city. "I have booked Hansraj into a room on the third floor," said Samrat.

"So, what do you think? Will he talk?"

"I am not too sure. I had lured him to the hotel under false pretences. Hansraj is under the impression that some distant relative of his, who had gone abroad, is going to meet him here today."

Rajvardhan looked at Samrat, a grin breaking out on his face. "But why did you do that?"

Samrat shrugged as they got into the old and cranky lift that shuddered its way to the third floor. "He's an old retainer, his loyalty lies more towards Raja Gajanan's parents than with anyone else. He had been with the family even before Harischandra Gajanan was born."

Rajvardhan sighed. "Do you really think the man would talk?"

"I think so, Raj. He would talk if he's convinced that Harischandra Gajanan might be in trouble. I have got information that Hansraj knows every single secret of the family; every skeleton that's hiding in their closet. I thought it best to wait for you before questioning him since I didn't want to lose him."

Rajvardhan nodded. "Thanks, Samrat. You're right. So, let's go see if we can make him talk."

Samrat knocked on the door of room no. 312. An old man opened the door after three minutes. "It's you," he said, giving Samrat a toothless smile, "come in, come in. And who is it with you?" He eyed Rajvardhan with blurry eyes, looking him up and down. "Are you from a royal family, *sahib*?"

"This is Prince Rajvardhan Thakore from Udaipur."

"*Namaste Kunwarji!*" Hansraj brought both his hands together in greeting, the expression in his eyes turning wary. What could have Raja Gajanan done now? The old servant was sick and tired of his master's atrocities. He knew for a fact that Harischandra's mother had been heartbroken when she died, having no hope of her son having a change of heart from the evil ways that he pursued.

The two men walked into the room before Samrat offered the only chair to Rajvardhan, standing against the wall, his arms crossed in front of him.

"Please sit down," said Rajvardhan, looking at Hansraj and pointing to the bed.

"*Ji Kunwarji*. What can I do for you?"

Rajvardhan spoke kindly to the old man, asking about him as well as his family, Hansraj answering all his questions honestly.

"Hansraj, let me be upfront, I need some help from you." Rajvardhan looked deeply into the old man's eyes.

"*Ji!*" What help could the Thakore Prince want from him? Hansraj turned to look at Samrat. "You told me that Mahendar was coming to see me."

"I know that's what I told you, Hansraj. But…"

Rajvardhan interrupted, "I had given instructions to Samrat not to reveal that I will be visiting you." He did not want Hansraj to lose confidence by finding out that Samrat had lied to him. The man would not mind if the instructions had come from him since he was royalty.

And Rajvardhan was right. Hansraj did not think there was anything amiss in the prince having given such an instruction. The old man nodded now, waiting for Rajvardhan to continue.

This was the first time Samrat was working with royalty and he was fascinated by the kind of loyalty they garnered from old servants. Hansraj's behaviour verged on slavish. The thought was followed by a doubt. If he was so loyal, would he spill the beans on Raja Gajanan? A small scowl darkened the detective's brow. It was an open secret that Akila Gajanan—Harischandra Gajanan's second wife—had been murdered. Even the local police, the older ones, knew about it. The problem was getting an eyewitness who was ready to testify in court. When he had found out that, at sixty-two, Hansraj was the oldest living servant in the royal household of Indore, Samrat had zeroed in on the man and got him away from the palace with his cock-and-bull story. He had had Hansraj's family inform the head servant at the palace that Hansraj had had to leave town urgently for the funeral of a relative.

"You have been working with the Gajanan royals since when?"

"I was ten when I went to work in the palace." There was pride in Hansraj's face and voice when he replied to Rajvardhan's question.

"Do you remember those days?"

"Of course. How could I forget? The Raja and Rani used to treat me like their own child. They gave me food from their own table. The Rani even taught me to read and write in Hindi. They loved me a lot." There were unshed tears in the old eyes.

"So, you were there when Harischandra Gajanan was born."

"*Ji!* The celebration went on for a whole month when the heir was born. I have never seen the Raja and Rani happier than at that time, ever before or after."

"Why is that? They must have only got happier, right? As Harischandra grew up?"

Hansraj shook his head sadly. "*Kunwarji,* the Raja and Rani had the most difficult time bringing up Raja Harischandra. He was not just wild, but violent. At least three horses got lame and had to be put to death before the present Raja learned to ride." Hansraj sighed. He had not spoken about all this to anyone other than his wife. But Rajvardhan Thakore was a prince. And royalty always stuck together. So, he did not find the questions odd nor had difficulty answering them.

"Why did Raja Gajanan divorce his first wife?"

"Princess Sitara?" Hansraj's face was sad when he thought of the young woman who had come to the palace as Harischandra's wife. She had been barely sixteen and delicate to a fault. "She couldn't give the Raja, who was a prince those days, a child. That's why he divorced her."

"What about otherwise? Were they happy with each other?"

Hansraj recalled those times when the Princess used to come down for her meals with dark bruises on her fair face. She was always covered from neck to heel with long blouses and saris. He had had his doubts and he had heard whispers. He had also not failed to notice the pain on the older royal couple's faces as they eyed their daughter-in-law with pity in their eyes. Oh, what was the use?

He looked at the prince who sat on the chair in front of him. Always used to obeying orders, he had never crossed the wish of any royalty. But this was the first time, anyone from outside the Gajanan family was asking him questions. Should he answer honestly? But then, how could he not? He could not even question the prince about the reason for his queries.

With a deep sigh, Hansraj said, "Not really, *Kunwarji*."

"Why do you think so?"

Hansraj felt ashamed, as if he was the one who had committed the heinous crime of harming the gentle princess. His voice was a hoarse whisper as he answered, "He used to beat her up, a lot. There were bruises on her face. I have noticed on those rare occasions when she stepped out of their rooms."

"What about Akila Gajanan?"

Hansraj blanched. He raised his hands in front of his chest and brought them together. "Can I please go back to the palace, *Kunwarji*?" If Raja Harischandra Gajanan found out that he had told the truth—that she had been pushed over the parapet wall from the third floor of the palace, to fall to her death on the rocks below—he would murder Hansraj.

"Soon, Hansraj. I have a reason for asking you these questions. Don't you want the old Raja and Rani's souls to attain peace?" Rajvardhan asked the old retainer gently.

Hansraj nodded his white head slowly up and down, a sorry expression on his face.

"Didn't Raja Harischandra Gajanan hurt them badly?"

A tear rolled down a withered cheek as Hansraj looked at Rajvardhan pathetically, the Adam's apple bobbing in his throat. He shook his head again. "Raja Harischandra murdered his own father, giving him poison." He broke down, falling on the bed to cry his heart out. "Rani *sahiba* died barely a week later, due to a broken heart."

Rajvardhan turned to look at Samrat and was relieved to see that he had recorded the whole conversation on his smart phone. They waited for Hansraj to calm down.

"Hansraj, are you ready to go live at the Thakore palace with your family? That's the only way I can keep you all safe."

Was there a choice? The old man nodded slowly, feeling only relief. He had kept the secret buried deep within his heart, not telling a soul. The Rani had known that her own son had killed her husband and had told Hansraj herself. This was the first time in fourteen years that Hansraj had spoken about it.

Rajvardhan and Samrat made arrangements for Hansraj and his wife to move to Udaipur immediately. The old man's daughters were both married and lived in some rural area that was not easily accessible. Rajvardhan was not too worried about them since he planned to get a warrant out for Gajanan in the next few days.

His phone rang just as he got into the car with Samrat, on his way back to the airport. "Hey!" It was Princess.

"Raj, where are you?"

"On my way to the airport in Indore."

"What?" Chitrangada yelped. "What are you doing there?"

Rajvardhan grinned. " I will tell you soon. We'll have to talk later."

"There's someone with you."

"That's right."

"You don't need to talk. Just listen, okay?"

"Sure."

"I love you, my darling Prince. I can't wait to get my hands on your body. Okay, maybe my lips too. I plan to…"

Rajvardhan grunted, his body tightening as she continued to make verbal love to him on the phone, refusing to disconnect as she gave a prolonged description of what she planned to do with his body.

"Princess, I need to go. Shall I give you a call soon?"

"What? That's a cold reaction to what all I've been telling you! Come on, Raj. You can tell me what you think of my plans." Her voice shivered with laughter as she imagined his discomfiture.

Rajvardhan managed to get out of the car at Departures and waved Samrat off before barking into the phone. "Just you wait, my Princess, till you get within touching distance. I'll show you."

"Promises, promises," Chitrangada gurgled. "Actually, the reason I called is that I need to go away for two days. I have a meeting set up with a client in Vadodara. I'm leaving tomorrow morning."

"Shit!" He paused for a minute, his mind working furiously, before asking, "Where are you staying?"

"I need to find out. The client is doing the booking."

"Tell them that you have your own accommodation. I'm booking us into ITC's Welcomhotel right now. I'll see you there tomorrow evening."

"Is that an order, Prince Thakore?"

"You bet it is. You'd better be prepared to deliver on your promise. I only hope my body can hold up till then," he grumbled.

She laughed outright. "Got to you, did I?"

"You have tied me up in knots, Princess, from the moment you stopped my car in the middle of that street in Zurich," he growled.

"Do you think a couple of nights in Vadodara will cure you of that ailment?"

"Not completely. But it sure will help. And hey, Princess, I love you."

"I adore you, my Raj."

"Raj!" Chitrangada flew into his arms the moment he entered their suite in Welcomhotel.

He hugged her close to his heart. "How was your day, sweetheart?"

"Perfect," she said, kissing him on his cheek. "To tell you the truth, I don't really know what I said to my client as I was only thinking of you."

Desire flared in his eyes as he looked down into her lovely face. "You are crazy, you know?"

"Yeah, I know. I'm crazy about you." She kissed him then, not letting him talk.

"I need a bath, love," said Rajvardhan when they finally came up for air.

"The bathtub is big enough for two," she said, fluttering her eyelashes at him suggestively.

Rajvardhan laughed, lifting her up in his arms. "Then what are we waiting for? Show me the way."

Chitrangada pointed in the direction of the bathroom with her left hand while she held on to his neck with her right arm, bending down to nibble his earlobe, sighing with pleasure as she traced the shape of his ear with her tongue.

Rajvardhan let her go on the carpeted bathroom floor before opening the taps to fill the bathtub and adding cologne scented bath salts generously to the fast-filling water. They helped each other undress, slowly and torturously, stopping for a kiss and a bite again and again.

Chitrangada ran both her hands over his chest, her palms tickled by the brush of crisp hair, rejoicing in the freedom to touch him. She pressed a wet kiss to a flat male nipple before taking a bite of it, making him groan long and loud.

He pulled her close to his aroused body, pressing his pelvis against her abdomen. "You feel so good in my arms."

"Mmm…" Chitrangada kissed her way down his chest, all the way down to his washboard abs, taking small bites of his ribs, following it up with strokes of her tongue.

Rajvardhan gathered a fistful of her hair and tried to pull her up. Only, she refused to be distracted.

"I want to taste you, Raj." She went down on her knees, her tongue working around his navel now.

"The bath is full now, Princess. Let's get into it." Rajvardhan gritted his teeth, his manhood twitching as it swelled harder than ever.

"In a minute." She refused to be distracted as she rubbed her cheek on his pubis, loving the feel of the crisp, dark hair. She turned her head to kiss his shaft, grinning when she heard his desperate groan.

"Do you want to kill me, woman?"

"Does intense pleasure kill a man?" She asked cheekily, lifting her head to look up at his tortured face.

"Very funny. Come into my arms now." He tried to pull her up once again, only to be thwarted.

Rajvardhan's eyes went wide in astonishment when she took the tip of his manhood in her mouth and sucked on it gently at first and vigorously afterwards.

"Princess!" moaned Rajvardhan, the hand in her hair pushing her closer to his body instead of trying to pull her up.

She continued to play with him for a few more moments, her soft hands tracing the shape of his muscular legs.

On the verge of exploding, he pulled her up, dragging a long, slim leg around his waist before thrusting into her deeply, making her cling to his hard shoulders for dear life as he pounded into her, again and again, before he felt her come apart, joining her in the celebration almost immediately afterwards.

Pressing his forehead to hers, he whispered, "Thank you, my love."

"For what?" she asked, grinning at him as she slid into the bathtub, her hand in his, "for having the most fun in my life?"

He sat inside the tub, pulling her on to his lap, his hands cupping her full breasts. "You enjoyed that, did you?"

"Totally." She pressed her back to his chest, her hands holding his arms, her head thrown back on his shoulder as she revelled in the leisurely strokes of his manly hands on her twin mounds. "That feels so good, Raj," she moaned even as she felt him kissing his way down the back of her ear to her neck and her shoulder.

They had a leisurely bath, making love in the water, until it turned cold. Chitrangada was half asleep when Rajvardhan got out to lift her out of the tub, wrapping a towelling robe around her. He took a towel and wiped her dry before drying himself.

"Have you had dinner?" she asked, remembering suddenly.

He laughed. "Yes, on the flight."

"Good." She was fast asleep the moment her head touched the pillow.

Rajvardhan held her, her back spooned against his front and breathed deeply of her scent. A smile on his face, it was not all that long before he fell asleep as well.

They both were up early the next morning and ordered breakfast in the room as Rajvardhan brought her up-to-date on what he had been doing over the past few days.

Chitrangada stared at him, her jaw wide in astonishment, as he told her about his meeting with

Sitara Gaekwad and Hansraj. She got up to hug him. "You have been working so hard, for my sake."

Ruddy colour rushed into Rajvardhan's face. "Don't be silly. I'm doing it for very selfish reasons. I want you for myself."

"Aww." She kissed him on a rough cheek. "Am I glad that I ran out on my bodyguards in Zurich! I would never have met you otherwise."

He turned his head to capture her lips with his and kissed her deeply.

After breakfast, he took out his phone and opened the photo gallery to show her a picture of a woman.

"Who's this?" Chitrangada stared at the picture. There was something familiar about the woman… or was it a *transgender*? It was a close-up shot. The woman was wearing a large, round *bindi* in between her thick, but well-shaped eyebrows. It was bright red in colour. Her eyes were thickly outlined with kohl, making their expression intense. Her generous lips were painted with a brilliant red lipstick that should have jarred but seemed to suit her face. Her dark hair was neatly oiled and brushed back, parted in the middle, to be gathered into a thick plait that she wore on her right shoulder. She wore chunky gold earrings and a clip-on nose screw. A rough cotton sari covered her large chest while thick hair covered her arms. Looking closely, Chitrangada noticed the hair on the top of her chest, above the sari and blouse. She turned to look at Rajvardhan and asked, "Is she a *hijra*?"

He nodded, a mysterious smile on his face.

"Why are you smiling?" She turned to look at the picture again. Why did the face seem familiar? She shook her head. Something was fishy.

"What? Don't you want to know who that is?"

She bit her lip, studying the picture once again before turning to look at his mischievous face. "Not really. Should I?"

He shrugged, trying to take his phone back. "Well, if you don't want to, then fine."

"Raj. Who is it? You know, she looks kind of familiar. But, I'm unable to place a finger on..." Chitrangada frowned in concentration, trying to remember where or when she had seen the woman in the photo. "What's her name?"

"Shikandi."

She shook her head. The name did not ring a bell. But... she turned to glare at his laughing face. "What's so funny? Why don't you just let me in on your joke?"

"You've been sleeping with me since a while now. You know every inch of my body, even better than I do. You still..."

"Raj, you bastard. It's you." Chitrangada squealed, jumping on him as he roared with laughter. The two of them rolled on the bed, howling with mirth for a long time. "But why?"

"I told you that I plan to be a part of your entourage when you visit Gajanan, didn't I?" He continued when she nodded, light dawning in her gaze. "This is the idea I came up with. If you couldn't recognise me, I'm confident that neither Gajanan nor your father will."

The light in her eyes diminished to be replaced by hurt. "You still don't believe my father."

"Your father deposited Gajanan's cheque and the money is credited to his account now." Rajvardhan's face was expressionless when he uttered those words.

"Oh Raj." Chitrangada buried her face in his chest, refusing to break down, even while she felt so betrayed.

18

"Shikandi, so glad you could come at such short notice." Chitrangada greeted her lover who was disguised as a transgender when he arrived at the Vasudeva palace. "Dad, this is Shikandi. She works for Yashodhara. I'm borrowing her for a few days so that she can accompany us to Harry's palace. And Shikandi, this is my father, Raja Bikram Vasudeva."

"*Namaste Raja sahib!*" Shikandi, taller than the Raja by at least three inches, bent down at the waist, bringing her hands together in a respectful greeting.

Bikram frowned, not acknowledging the greeting. "What was the need, Chitra?"

"Dad, you know how Harry is. I thought it's better if I had someone on my side. Don't you agree?" She decided to be as honest as possible while she did not really care what her father thought. Why should she, when he so obviously had no love lost for her?

Though he did not care for the idea, Bikram couldn't say anything. He was supposedly following Rajvardhan's idea. His daughter did not know that he had made his own alternate plan, having deposited Raja Gajanan's cheque. He had also spoken to Gajanan about bringing the wedding forward to the Sunday of their visit. Harischandra had been only too thrilled by the idea and had agreed to make all the arrangements.

So, let Chitrangada bring whoever she wanted. She was going to be Harischandra's wife by Sunday afternoon. And he, Bikram, would become the father-in-law of the billionaire Raja Gajanan at the same time.

Now, he nodded to Shikandi, not saying anything. He turned away abruptly, not noticing the wink his daughter gave her new servant.

The three of them left on Friday morning, along with a couple of other servants and a horde of luggage by the private jet that Raja Harischandra had sent for them. While Chitrangada had packed only one suitcase that carried all the changes of clothes she would need for the long weekend, her father seemed to have three suitcases, big ones at that. She decided not to question him as she was beyond caring now. What she did not know was that Bikram had packed most of her jewellery—Vasudeva heirlooms, her mother's jewellery that Chandrika's parents had given her at the time of their wedding, as well as those gifted by Harischandra— along with a trousseau of sorts. After all, he was going to give her hand in marriage to the Raja of Indore.

Harischandra Gajanan walked up and down the main hall of his palace, impatient for the arrival of his bride-to-be and her entourage. He had not been with a woman for the past two weeks as he couldn't imagine taking another in the place of Chitrangada Vasudeva. He smiled broadly at his own reflection in the floor-to-ceiling mirror fitted into an antique wooden frame, a maniacal expression in his eyes as he visualised making her his, his body growing hard at the thought.

The marriage was to take place on Sunday. But that did not mean that he planned to wait to tie the knot. Harischandra Gajanan never played by the rules. He smacked his lips thinking of all the plans that he had in place for Chitrangada's arrival. He did not think that her father would have a say in anything. He equated the man to a dog. He had thrown enough meat to Bikram and that should keep him quiet.

Gajanan went to the entrance of the main hall when he heard the arrival of two cars. A servant was opening the back door of the limousine that had been the first to arrive and out stepped Chitrangada, shining like a bright ray of sunlight, wearing a beautiful, blush pink sari in silk, gold jewellery on her ears, neck and wrists.

She brought both her hands together and said, "*Namaste* Raja Harischandra."

He threw an arm around her shoulders and gave her a hug, thrusting his throbbing pelvis against her slender body, eager to make her aware of his need. "Harry, my dear. You must call me Harry."

"And you must call me Chitra."

"But, of course."

Just as he was going to kiss her on her lips, Gajanan saw Shikandi get out of the car from the other side. His eyes widened with shock. Who or what was this?

Chitrangada noted the direction of his gaze and bit her lip to hold back her smile, her eyes dancing with mirth as they met Shikandi's. "Shikandi, come here and meet Raja Gajanan." She turned to her betrothed and said, "Harry, this is Shikandi. She is here to take care of my needs. You don't know what all she's capable of. She can play maid as well as secretary." She did not add that Shikandi was also her bodyguard.

"Is she a *hijra*?" Harischandra asked the question softly, fascinated by the tall transgender walking towards him. He felt a strange attraction towards Shikandi.

"Yes, a proud one at that."

"You are welcome to the Gajanan palace, Shikandi."

"*Namaste Raja sahib*." Shikandi, who towered over Gajanan, bent almost double to greet him in a guttural voice.

The voice stroked Gajanan's nerves, exciting him thoroughly. He had a grand visual of a threesome in bed, himself between Chitrangada and Shikandi, his body shuddering in delight.

"Harry, thank you so much for inviting us over." Bikram's voice interrupted Gajanan's vision, bringing him back to reality.

With a frown at the intrusion, he nodded his head in an absentminded fashion, saying, "Welcome to my palace, Bikram," with a total lack of enthusiasm.

But Bikram did not mind. He had already received three crore rupees from the Raja of Indore. What did it really matter how he treated him? As long as he still wanted to marry Chitrangada, everything was hunky dory. And he was going to receive the final payment of two crores way earlier than originally planned.

Chitrangada insisted that Shikandi would share her suite of rooms. She made a servant from Gajanan's household place a large bed in her bedroom for her servant's use.

"Why another bed, Princess? I can manage to sleep on the floor." Shikandi appealed to Chitrangada, her eyes gleaming with mischief.

Soft colour ran up Chitrangada's cheeks as she shook her head. "Yashodhara will never forgive me if I don't care for your comfort," she insisted.

Shikandi shrugged, helping the servant carry the bed into the room. Once the servant left, Shikandi went around the room, checking every nook and crevice.

"What are you doing?"

"Checking for hidden cameras."

"Aren't you being over cautious?" There was shock in Chitrangada's gaze as they met Shikandi's.

"I can't take enough precautions with that man. He's capable of anything. I don't know if you noticed. But he's lusting after not just you, but me too."

"Stop it, Raj. That's sick." Chitrangada gagged.

"Sorry for being insensitive, Princess. And the name is Shikandi. Never forget." Shikandi gave her a stern look of warning.

"I can't wait for the weekend to be over."

"Tell me about it." Shikandi had found not just one, but four cameras hidden in different parts of the room. But he did not share the information with Chitrangada as he could see that she had more than enough to digest as of now. He had to somehow convince her to get used to dressing up in the bathroom. He had scouted that room and found it clean of hidden devices.

Harischandra Gajanan had gone to his room to change for lunch. He stopped at the table in front of his bed, where four screens showed him the different angles of his betrothed's bedroom. The plan was for him to see everything happening in Chitrangada's bedroom even while he lay down on his bed. Just now, he was delighted to see that Shikandi, the transgender, was going to share her mistress's room. He was in for pure entertainment tonight for sure. Though there was not much happening except for the servant unpacking Chitrangada's suitcase and storing everything in the wardrobe. Shikandi had not unpacked her suitcase that she left in one corner of the room, close to her bed.

Why weren't they changing? He swiftly removed the clothes he was wearing, turning again and again to check out the screens, just in case he missed something.

He had dismissed Bhaktavar who also played valet. He did not want his Man Friday to have a peek at the screens. That was for his private entertainment only.

Pushing the buttons of his white dress shirt into their buttonholes, Harischandra turned to look at the screens once again and was disappointed to see Chitrangada walking out of the bathroom, draped in another sari, a turquoise silk. Why had she dressed in the bathroom when there was a big enough bedroom with a full-length mirror for her use? His face brightened almost immediately. Maybe she did not want to change in Shikandi's presence. All said and done, how could she, considering that the servant wasn't exactly a woman?

Tch! Why hadn't he thought of having a camera fixed in the bathroom?

He watched Shikandi help the princess wear her jewellery and also with her hair, her large hands deft as they worked on Chitrangada. His loins throbbed with excitement. He had to have both of them; and soon too.

During lunch, Shikandi stood at a respectable distance behind Chitrangada's chair and saw to her needs. What thrilled Harischandra was that, sitting opposite his bride-to-be, both Chitrangada and Shikandi were in his line of vision. *Aren't I so lucky!* he thought, eyeing them with pleasure as he sipped on his wine.

"I must compliment your cook, Harry. The food is delicious, the lamb cooked to absolute perfection," Bikram Vasudeva told his host.

Raja Gajanan gave a royal nod, not taking his eyes off the two women, well, one woman and one transgender. "I hope you are enjoying your meal, Chitra?" he asked solicitously.

"Oh yes, Harry. I agree with Dad. Everything is simply delicious, just as he says." Chitrangada nibbled at the food, pretending to relish her meal while her stomach curdled in anxiety. A shiver danced down her spine as she acknowledged that she simply hated the vibes of the Gajanan palace. The place appeared to be seeped in dark energies. She felt a strong urge to just get up and run away. Only Shikandi's powerful presence kept her from doing just that.

Harischandra's plan to get her alone was thwarted immediately after lunch. Chitrangada got up from the table to hold a hand to her head. "I need to rest, Harry. I'm really sorry for being such poor company. But I have a headache. I'll be alright once I am rested. Will you please excuse me?"

Gajanan eyed her, a malicious glint in his steel grey eyes as he studied her. Was she a weakling? He mentally shook his head. He did not really think so. She was probably just tired after her work week. All that will stop once she was his wife. She would never need to lift a finger to do any work. She could spend all her time in entertaining him. That conclusion brought a smile to his countenance as he nodded his head. "You do that, Chitra. Shikandi, you probably need to give the princess an oil massage to make her feel better. After she wakes up, of course," he told the servant before turning again to Chitrangada. "I want you to feel fresh this evening, Chitra. I have organised some special entertainment that I don't want you to miss. Now, Bikram and I will retire to the library to play a game of cards. Are you coming, Bikram?" He raised a supercilious brow at his future father-in-law.

"Of course, Harry. It would be a pleasure." Bikram immediately got up from the dining table and followed Gajanan like a puppy dog.

"You must have your lunch, Shikandi, before you return to my room." While Chitrangada's voice was authoritative, her eyes begged an apology that she had kept Rajvardhan waiting while eating her own lunch.

"Sure, Princess. I'll see you as soon as I finish lunch."

Chitrangada had no headache and she definitely didn't want to lie down on her bed. But she had needed an excuse to escape Harischandra's presence. Why hadn't her father told him immediately that they wanted to cancel the engagement? Isn't that what he had promised to do? Then again, Rajvardhan had said that her father had encashed Harischandra's cheque. What were her father's intentions? And how was Rajvardhan going to thwart them?

By now, she really had a headache coming on. Would she survive the night in the Gajanan palace? She had seen the expression in her *fiancé's* eyes.

He could not wait to get his hands on her. That was for sure. Damn it all!

And why had Shikandi insisted that she changed her clothes only in the bathroom? Had she found any hidden camera? If she had, Shikandi had not shared that information with her. Chitrangada turned from the window when she heard her door open and was relieved to see Shikandi entering the room.

"I'm scared, Raj." She ran across the room, eager to throw herself in his arms.

Shikandi raised a hand to stop her. "Stay away, Princess. Not here."

Chitrangada stopped in her tracks, barely a foot away from Shikandi, giving her a reproachful look. "Why?"

"There are cameras, four of them, at least."

Chitrangada frowned. "Why didn't you tell me before?"

"You had enough on your plate, and I didn't want to pile everything together."

She glared at him. "So considerate of you, Raj. But tell me, what the hell are we doing here? I don't think Dad is going to tell him that the engagement is off."

Shikandi nodded. "I'm glad you are aware of it now."

"Well, it's as obvious as the nose on my face now."

"Don't be bitter, sweetheart. It doesn't suit you." Rajvardhan aka Shikandi gave Chitrangada a wink, hoping to lighten the situation. He needed less than twenty-four hours before the commissioner of police came to the palace with Gajanan's arrest warrant. Both Sitara and Hansraj had recorded their statements in the presence of the magistrate and they had put together a watertight case against the Raja of Indore. It was a waiting game and had held good so far. Tonight, was crucial though. His main worry was to keep Chitrangada safe from Gajanan.

"Raj…"

"The name is Shikandi."

"Okay, Shikandi. I need a kiss, now, or I might just die." Let him come up with a way. She felt like picking up a fight. Who better than Rajvardhan to quarrel with?

Shikandi gave her an amorous look, ensuring that she herself was not facing any of the cameras. "Why don't you lie down, Princess? And allow me to give you the massage that Raja Gajanan ordered?"

She blushed. "I'd so love that. It's just that there's one, no, let me see, there are four issues. I don't want to be caught on camera, lying down naked and being given a massage." Her voice was highly sarcastic as she glared at him in frustration. She would have loved the massage, would have enjoyed his big hands all over her body.

"You are mistaken, Princess. We can't make a mess on the bed. I have arranged for a massage table to be put up in the bathroom. Do tell me when you are ready."

Her colour deepened when she looked into his twinkling brown eyes, reading the desire there. "In half an hour? It's barely an hour since I had lunch."

"Fine. Though it doesn't really matter since you had barely two spoonsful of lunch. Why, sweetheart?"

She went to sit on the bed. "Did you get a good lunch?" she asked. How did she forget to find that out? Chitrangada shut her eyes in horror before opening them again to look at him. "Raj, I'm terribly sorry. How did I not think of this? They must have treated you like a servant. Did they…?"

Shikandi shook her head, silencing Chitrangada effectively. "Princess, I repeat, call me Shikandi. And yes, I was fed well. You shouldn't worry about it," she said, her voice and expression gentle, "I have eaten worse. I eat to live, not the other way around."

"But still…" Chitrangada continued to look stricken.

"I think that massage will get rid of all your frustration." Shikandi grinned merrily at Chitrangada, walking towards the bathroom. "Let me check if everything is ready."

"Bastard! It'll serve you right when you are left totally frustrated after giving me that massage," Chitrangada growled, getting up to follow Shikandi into the bathroom.

Shikandi laughed outright. "Let's see about that."

19

Harischandra lay back on his bed, buck naked as he watched the monitor screens, a hungry expression on his face. It was about five in the evening. How could just watching a woman drying her hair be so fucking arousing? He had been hard even before Chitrangada arrived at his palace that morning. His manhood had been in a constant state of arousal from then on, the situation getting worse as time passed on.

He caressed himself now, almost drooling with pleasure as he watched Shikandi holding a container that emitted incense smoke, under Chitrangada's long hair. Unable to stop it any more, Harischandra masturbated right there on his bed, his excitement getting out of control.

Phew!

If watching the two of them could have this reaction on him, how was it going to be when all three went to bed together?

Harischandra had his plans in place for dinner. To begin with, it was going to be a twosome on the terrace. But right now, he decided that Shikandi was going to serve them dinner—Chitrangada and himself.

After wining and dining them, yes, Shikandi too, he planned to take them to bed. In all admiration for his own scheme, Harischandra got up to switch off the screens. He needed someone to come in and change the sheets. He also wanted Bhaktavar to help him get ready for dinner. Throwing a dressing gown around himself, he rang the bell for the servant.

Chitrangada arrived first on the terrace, escorted by a servant from the palace. Shikandi had promised to be there as soon as she could since she had some arrangements to make before arriving in time for the intimate dinner.

Princess Vasudeva stood at the parapet wall, watching the sun go down slowly behind the big trees that graced the palace compound. She was not to know that there used to be rocks on the ground at that particular point. All that had changed and the area was a green grass verge with several flowering shrubs, all appearing beautifully colourful.

She wondered where her father was, aware that it was going to be just Harischandra and herself for dinner, right here on the terrace. Wasn't she lucky that the Raja of Indore had decided to include Shikandi? The moment the servant who had brought the message to them regarding the evening plans left, Shikandi had laughed uproariously, throwing her head back.

"What's so funny about that?" Chitrangada scowled at the transgender.

"Can't you see what he's doing, your Raja Gajanan?"

"He's *not* my Raja Gajanan," Chitrangada snarled, angry sparks flying from her beautiful dark eyes.

Shikandi blew her a kiss, enjoying herself thoroughly, baiting the princess some more. "Wouldn't you have thought that he would have wanted you all alone for dinner? Your father obviously isn't going to be there."

Chitrangada nodded. "I heard the servant. You don't need to explain it all to me again. I'm not so foolish, you know."

"Foolish you definitely are not, my sweetheart." Shikandi laughed again, unable to stop herself. "If he wanted to have a private dinner with you, why would he include me?"

Chitrangada glared at Shikandi. "I don't know nor do I care. I'm just glad that I don't have to put up with him all alone. The truth is that I'll feel safer with you there." She raised a hand when Shikandi was going to interrupt, before continuing, "But feel free not to join us if you don't want to. I'm sure you have other, more important things to do. I am a karate blue belt. I can tackle him." She was totally miffed. What she did not realise was that it was sheer frustration that was making her so irritated.

The oil massage that Shikandi had given her had left Chitrangada completely dissatisfied. Shikandi had simply refused to change her avatar to Rajvardhan. "Not here in Gajanan's palace. I'm not suicidal, you know," she had insisted. But that had not stopped the transgender from giving the princess a thorough massage, driving her completely nuts.

And now, Shikandi was teasing her again. What Chitrangada did not realise was Shikandi was doing her best to keep the princess distracted from the danger she was in.

"Princess, why do you insist on picking up a quarrel with me? You know you aren't going to succeed. I don't intend being provoked, whatever you do. The focus now is to keep ourselves safe until help arrives. I don't plan to be distracted."

Chitrangada poked her tongue at Shikandi, unable to argue with the latter's logic. "I'm off to the terrace. You are welcome to join us if and when you are so inclined." She refused to let go of her anger.

"And by the way, a simple blue belt isn't going to keep you safe from the likes of the wily Gajanan."

"So, what's stopping you from playing my knight to the rescue?" she asked sarcastically.

"You know something? I can't wait for all this to be over before placing you across my knees and giving you the spanking that you so richly deserve." Shikandi swore, temper flaring in her heavily-kohled eyes.

A shapely eyebrow went up as Chitrangada stared at Shikandi, her anger having metamorphosed into a tingling excitement. "You, my dear Shikandi, make a lot of promises. I wonder when you plan to show some action. Are you all words or do you act too?"

"Get out, Princess, before I do something that jeopardises our purpose here."

"What if I refuse to go?" She challenged Shikandi.

"Maybe I can carry you to the terrace and place you in your darling *fiancé's* arms. I'm sure he'll appreciate my gesture."

"You wouldn't." Instead of shock, Chitrangada's eyes glowed in anticipation.

"Don't try me too hard. I just might. Now, go. I need to get something done before I join you on the terrace."

Seeing the purposeful expression in Shikandi's eyes, Chitrangada turned to leave. She walked all the way and stopped at the door, raising an index finger, gesturing to Shikandi to step closer. Confident that the cameras' range did not cover the doorway, the princess lifted her head to kiss Shikandi hard on the lips, thrusting her tongue deep within to stroke against hers. "Mmm… you taste awesome, my Shikandi." Chitrangada laughed.

"That was naughty, Princess." Shikandi grinned, lifting the *pallu* of her sari to wipe the traces of her red lipstick from Chitrangada's mouth. "You might want to repair your make-up."

"Shit!" Chitrangada smote her forehead. But she could not stop grinning back. "But it was totally worth it, Raj. I so missed kissing you."

"You, Princess," Shikandi shook her head, "are simply incorrigible."

"Would you like me to change? Become a yes-woman maybe?" Chitrangada gave Shikandi a challenging look, fluttering her eyelashes.

Shikandi threw back her head and laughed. "Not you, never. And thank God for that."

Now, Chitrangada stood there on the terrace staring at the sinking sun and thinking of her interaction with Shikandi aka Rajvardhan when she felt a hard arm going around her slender waist.

Shocked, she turned to see Harischandra standing right behind her. She had not even been aware that he had arrived.

"Hello, my lovely. I hope you had a good rest." Harischandra rubbed his hand over her waist, frustrated by the long blouse that she was wearing as he could not get to touch her skin. His eyes were on her heaving breasts, before he raised them to look at her gorgeous face.

"I did, Harry. You have a beautiful palace. I was just enjoying watching the garden." She tried to slide out of his arms, only to have them tighten around her. Before she could continue to distract him with her talk, he kissed her on her mouth.

Chitrangada gagged. Following so quickly on the kiss she had shared with Rajvardhan, it was a shock to find Harischandra's mouth on hers. The kiss was slimy and wet to say the least and she was completely revolted. When she refused to open her mouth, he bit her lower lip hard, so much so that the skin split and began to bleed. When she moaned in pain, she felt him thrust his lower body closer to her and she could feel him growing harder against her belly. With great difficulty, Chitrangada controlled her moans. She did not want to arouse him further. Where the hell was Shikandi?

A visibly excited Harischandra continued to maul her lips while he raised a hand to squeeze her breast, hard. Chitrangada gritted her teeth, hating his hands and mouth on her person, but not wanting to antagonise him. But she could not stop the small scream that left her lips when Harischandra pinched the tip of her breast, her eyes tearing up because of the intense pain. And the pain was not just physical. She was on the verge of connecting her knee to his groin when she heard Shikandi.

"Namaste Raja sahib, madam Princess!" Shikandi called out loudly the moment she entered the terrace. Her hands holding the ice bucket with two bottles of champagne trembled with the fury that shook her, her eyes blazing fire at Gajanan who held Chitrangada trapped in his arms. Shikandi did not fail to notice Chitrangada's lifted, bent knee despite the sari covering her. She smiled through her anger, walking forward to place the ice bucket on the circular table that had been set up in the middle of the square terrace.

When Gajanan turned to acknowledge Shikandi's presence, the transgender asked respectfully, "May I pour the champagne, your majesty?"

Harischandra held Chitrangada at his side, an arm around her waist, as he guided her towards the table. "Would you like some champagne, Chitra? I bought it from France some years ago and had saved it for a special occasion." He felt so satisfied when he noted her swollen mouth. The bleeding had stopped and he smacked his lips, still able to taste her blood, a proud smile on his face. He eyed Shikandi's tall figure at the same time. She was clad in another cotton sari, probably her signature style, appearing almost regal in the fading light of the setting sun.

Letting go of Chitrangada, Gajanan accepted the champagne flute and raised it in a toast. "To the most beautiful woman in my life, the one who's soon to become my wife." He smiled at Chitrangada, saying, "Drink up, Chitra," tilting his head and drinking the sparkling wine in a couple of swallows. "Pour me some more," he ordered Shikandi.

"Sure, your majesty," said Shikandi, her eyes gleaming as she topped his glass. She also turned a surreptitious glance towards Chitrangada to notice that she had but taken a couple of sips from her own glass. "May I serve you some starters, Princess?" Shikandi asked, eyeing her swollen lips with mounting anger, swearing mentally, *I am going to kill the bastard with my bare hands!*

Chitrangada looked at Shikandi, her face pinched, even as her chin trembled. Gritting her teeth, she said, "Could you, Shikandi? I'm so hungry."

Shikandi served a few pieces of the *paneer tikka* and *mutton kabab* on a plate and placed it in front of Chitrangada, before continuing to ply Gajanan with more champagne. When Chitrangada was about to lift her champagne glass to her lips, Shikandi flashed a look at Gajanan before taking the glass from her and replacing it with a glass of water.

Chitrangada stared at Shikandi, a look of enquiry on her face. The latter simply shook her head, saying nothing.

It was a little more than half an hour when Harischandra keeled over and fell on the terrace floor, out like the light.

Chitrangada's jaw dropped. "What happened? Don't tell me he's dead. That I could be so lucky!"

Shikandi laughed. "I had spiked the champagne," she said softly. "He'll be out for at least twelve hours."

"What if someone finds out?" Chitrangada looked up at Shikandi, her gaze wide and dancing with mirth, while she pressed her hands one on the other, over her mouth.

"And how will they do that? Unless you plan to tell them." She suddenly stepped close to Chitrangada, touching her lips with a gentle finger. "He has hurt you badly. Does it pain too much? I'm so sorry that I took longer than expected." There was remorse in her voice.

Chitrangada pouted her lips to kiss Shikandi's caressing finger. "Not anymore."

Shikandi moved away when she heard someone coming up the staircase and walked over to where Gajanan lay. "*Raja sahib, Raja sahib,*" she called out, patting the sleeping man's cheek a trifle too hard. Turning to see Bhaktavar followed by a servant carrying a tray with bowls of hot food, Shikandi said, "*Raja sahib* has fallen asleep. I think he has had too much to drink. We need to carry him to his room." Saying that, she dropped the Raja's head none to gently on the floor.

Bhaktavar rushed over to his boss and checked his pulse. It was beating steadily, though a mite faster than was regular. Convinced that he must be more drunk than usual, Bhaktavar instructed the servant to call two hefty men in their employ.

"Princess, you must come along with me," said Shikandi in her gentlest voice. "Bhaktavar, the princess is traumatised. I'll take her away from the scene. She has never seen anyone drink themselves under the table, ever before." Her voice was stern when she addressed Gajanan's Man Friday.

"I'm sorry, Princess Chitrangada. You must excuse Raja Harischandra Gajanan," said Bhaktavar in his most pacifying voice. "He has never been like this. This is the first time I have seen him unable to hold his drink."

Princess Chitrangada gave him a regal nod without uttering a word in reply. "Take me to my room, Shikandi. I think I'll have a quiet meal in my own quarters."

Bhaktavar did not notice when Shikandi lifted the Champagne bucket and carried it along with her, not wanting anyone to check the bottles, just in case.

Shikandi pulled Chitrangada into her arms the moment they turned around their corridor and held her close to her heart, stroking the princess's back rhythmically. It was a while before Chitrangada's racing heart calmed down. She lifted her face to Shikandi and said, "I want my Raj back, now."

"Done. Just give me ten minutes and I'll return Raj to you and that's a promise," said Shikandi.

Rajvardhan joined Chitrangada at the table that was spread with a lavish dinner. Chitrangada had locked the door behind the servant before Rajvardhan stepped out of the bathroom to jam the cameras. They sat down to eat the heartiest meal since they had arrived at the Gajanan palace.

"So, what's going to happen now?" Chitrangada asked him as she leaned her head on his shoulder.

"I am going to make love to you first," Rajvardhan declared, hugging her close. "Then, I'm going to keep a vigil through the night. Gajanan should not wake up, but I don't want to leave anything to chance. The police commissioner and his men will arrive by ten in the morning. Once Gajanan is arrested, we can leave the palace."

"You make it all sound so simple, Raj. Do you really think he will give up so easily?" Chitrangada gave him a worried glance before pressing her cheek to his.

"He won't," declared Rajvardhan. "Of course not. But then, he can't do much in the face of so much evidence that has been gathered against him. He's not above the law."

Bhaktavar sat next to Raja Gajanan watching him sleep. He was deeply worried about what was going to happen when his master woke up. Harischandra had been so looking forward to making love to his *fiancée*. He had spoken about it to Bhaktavar in detail, actually. But his plan had flopped when he got drunk so much to simply fall into a deep sleep. He was going to be terribly upset when he woke up. And if one considered past history, Bhaktavar knew that the Raja would turn violent, beating up anyone who came into his presence. But that still did not make the loyal Bhaktavar leave his sleeping master. So, he dozed, sitting right next to the bed on an upright chair.

20

It was twenty past ten in the morning when Harischandra opened bleary eyes. He turned first one way and the other, realising that he was in his bedroom. He looked up at the monitor screens and was disappointed to see that there was no one in Chitrangada's bedroom.

He turned his head to his right and noticed Bhaktavar snoring away softly as he sat on a chair, his head lolling to one side. "Bhaktavar," he called, his voice hoarse, his mouth and throat feeling dry. "Bhaktavar," he shouted with an effort, jerking the other man awake.

"You are awake, your majesty." Bhaktavar got up with a jerk to stand next to Gajanan, even as he surreptitiously checked the wall clock. 10.25 am.

"I don't remember getting into my bed, Bhaktavar. What is the time? Oh, and get me a glass of premium whiskey. I'm thirsty." Harischandra's voice was authoritative.

Bhaktavar squirmed. "May I please get you some water first?"

"Do what I say." Harischandra glared at his valet.

Bhaktavar rushed away and returned within a minute, carrying a tray with a glass of whiskey as well as a terracotta bottle full of water. Setting the tray on the bedside table, he said, "Please have some water first, your majesty. You must be parched."

"And how would you know that?" Harischandra paused midway to picking up the whiskey glass.

"*Rajaji*, you have been sleeping for a straight fifteen hours." Bhaktavar's expression was pathetic when he informed Harischandra that.

"What?!" Harischandra jumped out of his bed, lifted the terracotta bottle and drank the cool water from it thirstily. He placed the empty bottle down and snarled at his valet. "What happened?"

Bhaktavar gave his employer a worried look. Harischandra was capable of maiming if not killing the messenger. And what he had to say was definitely not good news. Not really having a choice, he spoke fast, "When I went to the terrace last evening, along with the servant carrying your dinner, you had fallen down and were fast asleep."

Harischandra shook his head as if to clear it. He remembered Shikandi pouring him glass after glass of the excellent champagne. Chitrangada had been sitting at the table eating, even while she sipped from her own glass. He could not remember anything after that. He looked at Bhaktavar unseeingly, a deep frown on his forehead. "Where are my guests?"

"Let me find out, *Rajaji*. I haven't moved from your side all night."

Harischandra gave him a small smile of appreciation, distracted by his own thoughts. If, by any chance, the wine had been drugged, then Chitrangada would also have gone to sleep, right? Unless… unless she had drunk but a few sips.

Light dawned on his face. Someone had given him a sleeping draught. "Hand me my dressing gown," he ordered, opening the bedside drawer, and removing his pistol. Wrapping the dressing gown over his pyjama pants and holding the gun hidden in his hand which he thrust into the gown's pocket, Gajanan walked swiftly out of his bedroom. He did not meet anyone on his way as he went to the head of the stairs. Looking down, he was surprised to see a dozen people sitting in the entrance hall.

"Well, well, to what do I owe the pleasure of all your company?" he called out, walking down the stairs. He was glad now that Bhaktavar had insisted that he drink the water instead of the whiskey he had preferred. He sure needed a clear head.

There was Bikram and Chitrangada, of course. But what was Prince Rajvardhan Thakore doing here? Did he not live in Udaipur? Harischandra kept the frown away from his face, not wanting anyone to read his mind. And who were the other men?

And, where was Shikandi? His temper built to a crescendo. He hoped for her sake that the *hijra* had not left the premises. She was the one who must have spiked his drink.

He went and sat on a sofa in the middle of the hall and checked out all his guests, one by one. "May I ask what you are all doing here, in my home, uninvited? And you, Thakore, I don't remember giving you an appointment." His voice was silky with menace.

Before Rajvardhan spoke, a tall man who had been sitting across Harischandra spoke up, his voice boomeranging in the cavernous hall that had a ceiling at a height of thirty feet. "Harischandra Gajanan, we haven't met before. I am the new police commissioner and have joined duty only last month. The name is Shikawat."

"And the purpose of your visit?" What did he care if it was the prime minister himself? This was his palace and home, damnit! People cannot just walk in when they pleased.

"I have a warrant for your arrest, Gajanan, for the murder of your father, Raja Digvijay Gajanan and your second wife, Akila Gajanan. There's also a complaint filed by your ex-wife, Princess Sitara Gaekwad that she had suffered torture at your hands during her brief marriage to you."

Harischandra had been steadily going red in the face as the police commissioner spoke. He got up with a jerk, removing the hand holding the pistol from his pocket. He pointed the gun at Shikawat, saying, "Get out of my home."

"I am warning you to co-operate, Gajanan. There are too many of us here and each one of us is armed. Forget about escaping, you won't be able to get out of this alive if it turns into a shooting match." Shikawat's voice was firm.

He would teach them, all of them. Gajanan glared his hatred at Bikram and his daughter before turning his angry gaze towards Rajvardhan. They all deserved to die. How had they found out all his secrets? How had they managed to gather evidence? And Sitara, his bitch of an ex-wife! She had seemed so innocent. She had never opened her mouth in all these eighteen years. How had they got her to open her trap?

These thoughts ran through Harischandra in the next few seconds before he came to a conclusion. He may be outnumbered. But he was not going to surrender without a fight. Training his gun towards the ceiling, he shot not once, but three times, up in the air.

Everyone other than the Raja looked up in horror as the massive chandelier made of wrought iron and glass, weighing two-hundred-plus pounds, made a terrifying noise as it broke from the ceiling and came crashing down, falling directly on Harischandra Gajanan.

Not aware of what he had done, the Raja laughed demonically at every one of his unwanted guests who had come to their feet in shock. Before he realised that it was not his gunshots that had brought them to their feet, Harischandra was knocked down, the weight of the chandelier crushing him underneath, glass shattering all over the hall, most of the pieces soaked with his blood.

Bhaktavar howled, beating his chest as he watched his master breathe his last. He was probably the only one who felt any kind of remorse at the monstrous Raja's death.

21

S ome weeks later…

It was four days after Prince Rajvardhan Thakore and Princess Chitrangada Vasudeva were married in a grand three-day ceremony at the Thakore palace.

They had decided to honeymoon at Ashvaraj Farms. Along with a team, Chitrangada had renovated two more rooms at the heritage structure for them to use. They appeared resplendent and perfect for the royal couple.

The newlyweds had just got back from a long ride in the evening, giving their horses their heads around the periphery of the one-hundred-square-kilometre farm.

Rajvardhan jumped off his horse before turning to his wife. "Need help?"

"Not really," she said, without making an effort to get down. "But I *want* you to lift me down." She looked deeply into his warm coffee brown eyes, her own crinkling with laughter, as she jumped into his waiting arms, throwing her own around his neck. "I love you, my Raj."

Still holding her up in his arms, he lifted his face for a kiss, not to be disappointed. Giving her a sharp slap on her bottom, he let her slide down his arms, saying, "Let's go have a bath."

"Shall we go swimming in the lake?"

"In the nude?" he dared her, a lifted eyebrow, and a naughty smile on his face.

"I would love that. But are you sure?"

"It's twilight. No one will come near the lake. You know how they all like to watch TV." There were three families who lived on the farm, including Kanhaiya and Suruchi, as Rajvardhan was on an expansion spree. He had also hired two more stable hands who came in the morning and must have left by now.

With excitement leaping in her heart, Chitrangada took her husband's hand, giving him a nod.

"Let me go get a couple of towels and robes," he said, moving towards the palatial house in a jog, Chitrangada following him at a leisurely pace.

He joined her even before she reached the entrance and the two of them took a turn towards the lake that was about half a kilometre from the house.

It was almost dark when they stripped off their clothes, leaving them on the bank along with the towels, before walking into a shallow end of the lake.

The water was perfect, having turned warm during the day, making it a pleasure to swim in. They swam for about twenty minutes before she felt his arms going around her from behind. She trod water to lean against him, giving a sigh of pleasure when she felt his lips at her neck. She held to his arms as they crossed over her breasts, revelling in their weight against her twin mounds.

Turning her head, she offered her lips to him. Rajvardhan accepted her invitation immediately to press his mouth to hers, thrusting his tongue deeply into her mouth, tracing the inner cavern with lazy strokes.

"Mmm… you taste so good," said Chitrangada, turning around to press her torso to his chest, enjoying the feel of the crisp hair against her silky breasts. She lifted a leg to wrap it around his lean waist, holding his hardened shaft in her right hand as she guided it into her body.

With a groan of satisfaction, Rajvardhan plunged into her, again and yet again, before they found their release together as one.

Burying her face into his shoulder, Chitrangada smiled. "You know, I had made some special plans for tonight."

"Why the past tense?" His hands splayed over her bottom as he held her lower body close to his.

"How much fun can we have on one given day?"

"As much as we want. So, what's this you have been planning?" He asked, tracing his lips down her jaw.

"You don't really believe I am going to tell you, do you?" Chitrangada tilted her head, giving him access to her throat as he stroked his tongue over a fast-beating pulse.

"So, you aren't going to." He bent his head down to take a bite of her plump breast, making her moan with longing.

"You keep that up," she told him in a threatening voice as he closed his mouth over the turgid tip of her right breast, "and I might have to shift the surprise to tomorrow night."

His laughter fluttered against her breast as he moved his head to capture the other nipple, suckling on it deeply. It was a while before he let go of it to lift his head up and ask, "Are we on a ration?"

"Raj, we can't keep making love all the time."

"Says who?" he asked, taking her hand and placing it against his burgeoning loins. "This is our honeymoon. And before you ask, I plan to make my whole life one long honeymoon."

"Bastard." She punched him on his shoulder with her left hand, even as her right hand traced the shape of his manhood, latching her mouth to his and biting him hard.

"She-devil," he retaliated even as he shut his eyes in joy while she guided him deep within her, yet again.

Rajvardhan saw that it was three in the morning when he suddenly came awake. He was lying on his back, with his wife wrapped around him. She was sleeping on her side, her left arm hugging him, her left leg curling around his middle. His Princess loved to cuddle. He, who had never liked anyone near him while sleeping, had begun to love having her all over him each night. It had been so, even in Zurich.

"Are you awake?" she mumbled sleepily in his ear.

"Hmm…"

"Do you want to be surprised?" She moved to lie down the length of his body, her chin pressed on his chest.

He opened his eyes in a half slit and studied her eager face, his eyes coming alive with mischief. She looked so determined.

"Aren't we done with today's quota of sex?" he asked, his chest rumbling with laughter.

She gave him a mock frown, pretending to check the time on the bedside clock. "We haven't even begun today," she said, a serious expression on her face.

Rajvardhan burst out laughing, hugging her close. "So, surprise me."

She moved up his chest to kiss him hard on his lips, before sliding out of his arms.

"Where are you going?" He snagged her hand, refusing to let her go.

She turned around to give him a naughty look. "Patience, my prince."

He let her hand slide out of his, wondering what she was up to as he noticed her secretive expression.

She was back in a minute, carrying something in her hands.

"What's it?" he asked.

"Do you trust me?" she asked him in reply. When he nodded, she said, "Close your eyes."

Rajvardhan opened his eyes wider than before, staring at her in curiosity, an eyebrow up in query, as he checked out her bobbing breasts, lifting a hand to brush it across one.

"Raj, if you don't close your eyes, I might have to blindfold you," she said in a threatening voice.

"Oh okay." He grinned widely, even as he shut his eyes, his hand continuing to shape her breast, a thumb rubbing rhythmically against the swollen tip.

"And keep your hands away from me."

"Princess!" he protested, "I wanna touch you."

"Only when I tell you, not before," she said, a determined thrust to her chin.

He opened one eye to look at her. "What's this game?"

"I'm not going to tell you unless you listen to me." Chitrangada crossed her arms against her tingling breasts as she pretended to glare at her husband's mischievous face.

"Okay, okay." He raised his hands in a gesture of peace and shut his eyes once again.

Chitrangada walked swiftly to the head of the bed and tied two of his silk ties to the bars. She took his right hand in hers and tied the free end of one of the ties around his manly wrist in a loose knot. She did the same with his other hand.

Catching on with what she was doing, Rajvardhan lay back, a smile on his face. She did the same to his ankles, before going on her knees beside him on the bed.

And that is how the delightful torture began, the one that was his wife's surprise for him. She first trailed her hair all over him, beginning with his face and ending with his feet. "Don't open your eyes, Raj," she whispered, when he tried to take a peek at her.

"But, Princess, I wanna see you," he groaned when he felt her lips over every inch of his body.

"Where's your sense of adventure, Raj? Can't you see me in your mind's eye?" she gurgled, taking a bite out of his big toe, making him jump. His shaft was ramrod straight, standing up in invitation by the time Chitrangada gave him a body rub with her breasts, making him groan louder than ever.

He clamped his teeth over a breast tip, making her moan in hunger. "That feels so good, Raj."

"And what you are doing to me, my Princess, is simply terrific."

"You are liking it?"

"Too much," he said, running his tongue in circles over the nipple.

She moved away from his face, down his body, finally reaching his manhood and rubbing her breasts against him.

"Princess," he groaned, long and hard, "stop this right now and take me. Or I might just explode."

Laughing, she took his throbbing shaft and placed it at the entrance to her vagina and fell on him, riding him in a frenzy, her head thrust back as she reached out to the stars, her body trembling with the tremors building up within her. "Raaaaaaajjjj…" Chitrangada screamed as she came again and again, even as he lifted his body to thrust deep into her one last time before he exploded in a wild orgasm too.

Chitrangada fell on his chest, like a ragdoll, totally spent.

"Sweetheart, will you untie me now? I need to hold you." Rajvardhan was pleading by now, desperate to hug his wonderful wife.

With lethargic movements, she lifted her hands to untie the knots, releasing his hands, feeling glad when his arms moved around her, holding her close.

He kissed the top of her head, his hand brushing against her soft back. "You, my love, have always tied me in knots. But just now, you outdid yourself." He grinned at her when she lifted her head to look at him.

"Did you like my surprise?"

"Not like, my Princess, I loved it, too much. You are the best!"

"As are you, my Raj. I feel so free with you." She said, burying her face in his masculine shoulder.

THE END

REFERENCES

1. Indian Royalty: https://www.scoopwhoop.com

2. Horse breeding: https://en.wikipedia.org/wiki/List_of_horse_breeds

3. Snow polo: http://www.telegraph.co.uk/sport/othersports/polo/11372115/Snow-Polo-St-Moritz-World-Cup-2015-Huge-snowfall-slows-down-building-of-infrastructure-for-Cartier-Trophy.html

4. St Moritz: https://en.wikipedia.org/wiki/St._Moritz

5. Hotel Storchen, Zurich: https://storchen.ch/en/

6. Alden Suite Hotel Splügenschloss Zurich: http://www.alden.ch/en-gb

7. Polo match: https://en.wikipedia.org/wiki/Polo

8. Polo in India: https://en.wikipedia.org/wiki/Polo_in_India

OTHER BOOKS
BY
SUNDARI
VENKATRAMAN

THE THAKORE ROYALS
BOOK 1
The
MARRIAGE
PREDICAMENT
SUNDARI VENKATRAMAN

Princess Yashodhara Jadeja of Bhatewar isn't at all keen to get married. With her tarnished past, she knows that her married life would never be easy. But, between her father's Will and her mother's persuasion, she's left with no choice.

Prince Indrajeet Thakore of Udaipur agrees to meet Yashodhara as a prospective wife after his grandmother, Rajmata Santhini Devi, persuades him. While no cymbals crash at their first meeting, the couple grow to like and respect one another before they agree to tie the knot.

Both belong to royal families and both have responsibilities. Over and above all that, their marriage is plagued by a predicament, just as Yashodhara had expected. It looks like they can lead a happy married life only if the princess is willing to break a promise. Will she be able to do that? And will Prince Indrajeet continue to love her once he gets to know about her past?

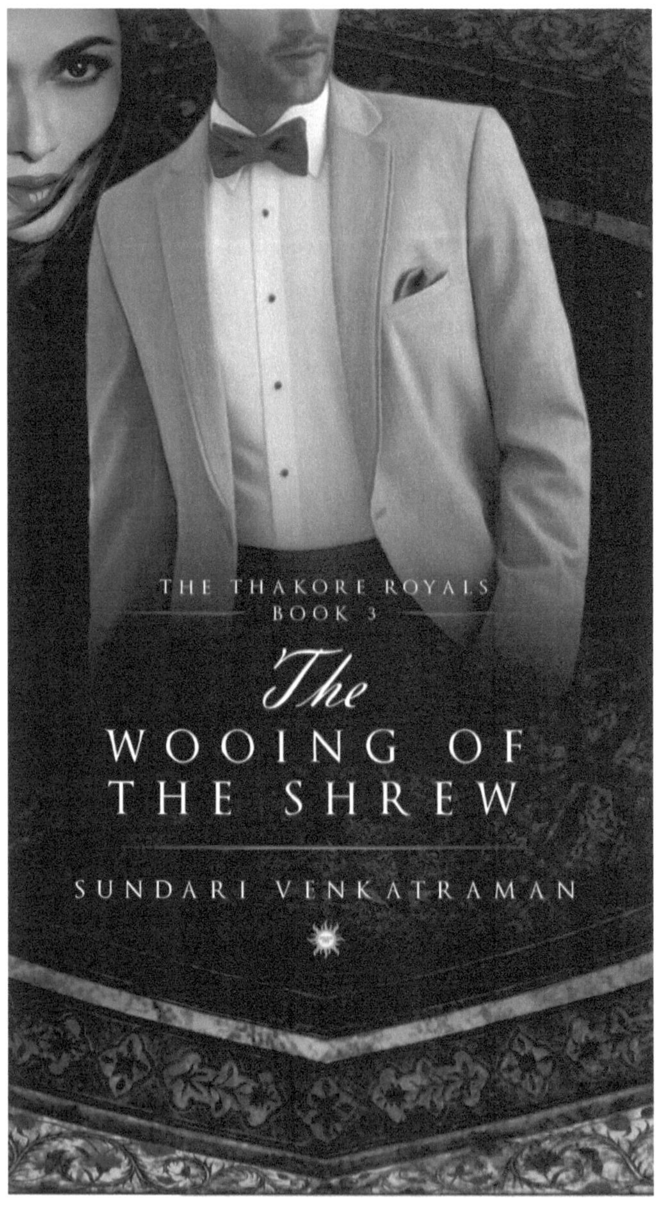

THE THAKORE ROYALS
BOOK 3
The
WOOING OF
THE SHREW
SUNDARI VENKATRAMAN

Dayanita Thakore is a prickly princess who doesn't care for the idea of any man getting close to her... until Prince Harshvardhan Singh Gaekwad turns up in her life.

Sparks fly even at their first meeting when the Princess of Udaipur clashes with the Prince of Baroda.

He falls in love with the fiery princess while she fights her attraction to him tooth and nail.

He woos her, beguiles her, cherishes her...

...while the princess feels that maybe he couldn't love such a tempestuous woman such as herself.

But before they could cross the great divide and get to know each other, something happens, something terrible that might just blow their lives apart.

Do they have a chance at a happily ever after?

Man Friday
SUNDARI VENKATRAMAN

Rituraj realises he's in love with the Gaekwad princess, Sitara Devi. The timing is slightly wrong though. Just ten minutes ago Sitara Devi married Harishchandra Gajanan. All of seventeen and nursing a badly bruised heart, Rituraj takes up boxing, hoping to build his strength and heal his wounded soul.

When destiny gives them a second chance, hope springs in his heart.

Rituraj grabs the opportunity of becoming Sitara's bodyguard-cum-assistant. He's the only man in her life but he's just her Man Friday. Since his father was merely an employee of Sitara's father, will he even be considered as a prospective life partner for the Gaekwad princess?

Sitara and Rituraj are crazily attracted to each other, yet they are unable to move forward. So where is the hitch? Why the fear in taking the relationship to the next level?

Class Barriers! Debauchery! Sexual Perversion!

It looks like 'Ne'er the twain shall meet'.

Read the book to find out if Sitara eventually gets together with her Man Friday.

Connect with Sundari Venkatraman here:

Notion Press: Sundari Venkatraman Books

Amazon: Sundari Venkatraman Books

Website: https://www.sundarivenkatraman.in

Facebook: Author Sundari Venkatraman

Twitter: @sundarivenkat

Instagram: @sundarivenkatraman

Email: sundarivenkat@gmail.com